Right Where They Belong

SUTTON SERIES BOOK 1

CHANTAL DeYoe

To Carol - Happy Reading!

Chantal DeYoe

LIVING OUT OUR CHRISTIAN FAITH PUBLISHING LLC

Copyright © 2024 by Chantal DeYoe

All rights reserved.

No part of this publication may be reproduced, distributed, or transmitted in any form or by any means, including photocopying, recording, or other electronic or mechanical methods, without the prior written permission of the publisher, except as permitted by U.S. copyright law. For permission requests, contact Living Out Our Christian Faith Publishing LLC.

The story, all names, characters, and incidents portrayed in this production are fictitious. No identification with actual persons (living or deceased), places, buildings, and products is intended or should be inferred.

Book Cover by Lynn Andreozzi

First Edition 2024

Table of Contents

Part One

1	1
2	5
3	9
4	18
5	28
6	39
7	57
8	63
9	80
10	84

11	96
12	107
13	122
14	131
15	144
16	149
17	166
18	176
19	181
20	188
21	198
22	202

Part Two

1	207
2	218
3	225
4	233
5	242
6	246
7	251

8	256
9	264
Part Three	
1	267
2	272
3	279
4	283
5	286
About the Author	300
Acknowledgements	302
Coming Soon!	303

1

One time each year, give or take, Corinne packed up her car and moved someplace new. She didn't have to; she just could.

Hopping about the country was so out of character for anyone in Corinne's family that they simply couldn't understand it. "If you're so eager to see the world, why don't you just travel?" they asked her.

"I am traveling," Corinne replied. "I'm just living there while I do it."

Last week she had turned in the key to her apartment in Phoenix and headed east. She had no particular destination in mind—she never did—but was certain she'd know it when she got there. She always did. After veering north and spending a few days with her family in Indianapolis, she was back on the road, headed east again, and coming into Columbus.

Corinne stopped for fuel and dug out the lunch her mom had packed for her. No matter how old she got, her mom always took care of her when she was home. She said a brief prayer of thanks for the food, and her mom, and took a bite of her sandwich. Next, she pulled up a map of Ohio on her phone. The roads were crazy, a spider web criss-crossing the state. She studied the whole thing, and several minutes later, when she had downed the last bite of her lunch, decided north was the way to go once again.

An hour later, she was deep in Ohio farm country. She had left the main roads and passed through gently rolling hills. Now the land was flattening, and she saw a sign proclaiming, *Sutton, 2 miles.*

It was just like any other roadside sign she'd ever seen, except that this one captured her attention. She contemplated this for a split second and then shrugged her shoulders. *Why not?* Maybe a small town would be nice. At any rate it would be a complete departure from every other place she'd lived.

She drove the two miles into town. *Definitely not frantic,* she thought. *Way less traffic. Could be a nice change of pace.* She parked on Main and surveyed the street. Each block was a solid mass of buildings on both sides; all connected and all occupied. That was a good sign. No high rises, of course. Maybe here she could live in an actual house! She backed out of her parking spot and continued exploring.

After an hour, she headed back toward the edge of town and the hotel she'd seen on her way in. At least she'd spend the night and see if the charm had worn off in the morning.

It hadn't. It was so quiet and peaceful overnight, Corinne couldn't believe it. She snagged a copy of the local newspaper and some cereal from the hotel's breakfast bar and began scouring the For Rent ads. Amazingly, there was a little house listed. She was shocked at how cheap it was. *Surely must be a dump,* she thought.

It wasn't. Turns out, housing just cost less in a small town. *Who knew?* Corinne signed the lease and got busy moving in.

"Moving in" for Corinne was mostly about finding inexpensive furniture and setting up her office workspace. She never relocated more stuff than she could fit in her car.

After six years of moving about the country, she was proud of the fact that she could still accomplish this.

Nevertheless, a new residence always deserved a good cleaning, so Corinne was still in the thick of it when lunchtime rolled around. She recalled the little diner she'd seen on Main Street and sought a phone number in the ancient, dog-eared book that had been left on the counter. Twenty minutes after calling in an order, she washed the residue of moving day off her face and hands, brushed her hair, and clipped it up into a loose twist. She slapped her sunglasses onto her face and headed out the door.

Another nice thing about a small town, you could get anywhere in just a few minutes. Corinne was liking it already. She parked her car and walked past a couple of store fronts down to the diner, pulled open the glass door, and stepped inside.

2

"Holy crap!"

Marcus gaped at the woman who'd just walked through the door of the diner. His hands froze halfway to his mouth, sandwich forgotten. The woman took off her sunglasses and propped them on top of her head. She glanced around the room and then walked to the counter. Marcus's heart was pounding. He could hardly breathe.

His friend chuckled and shoved a huge bite of burger into his mouth. He chewed for a few moments and then casually turned to have a look. The woman hadn't taken a seat, but instead was standing by the register.

Marcus was mesmerized. Although by what, he couldn't tell. No curves to speak of. Jeans and a t-shirt. Not even any make-up. Still though, there was something about her. "That woman," he said, "is going to be my next wife."

Daniel scoffed. "Oh, come on."

"No, I'm serious."

"Dude, you don't know anything about her."

"Oh, I will. Just give me time."

Daniel looked at the woman again as she was paying for takeout. "She's probably married," he said.

"Nope. No ring."

"How can you tell from here?"

"I can tell these things. It's a gift."

Daniel rolled his eyes. "Well, I don't think she's your type."

Marcus glared at his friend. "What do you mean, 'Not my type'?" He glanced at the woman again. "She's perfect."

Daniel shrugged. "Maybe so; she looks like a nice girl." He leaned forward and whispered, "Like I said, not your type." He grinned at his friend and took another bite.

"Screw you," Marcus muttered.

"Besides," Daniel said, the words garbled through the food, "I've never seen her before. She's probably just passing through."

"No way." Marcus pounced. "She picked up an order, which means she called it in. Nobody just 'passing through' ever goes through Sutton, and even if they did, they'd never find Maddie's Diner online to call in an order." He snapped his fingers and pointed at Daniel. "She's new in town."

Daniel shook his head. "Impressive, Counselor. You better hope you're right." He lifted his chin toward the door, where the woman had just exited.

"Oh, shit. I've got to get her name. Maddie!" Marcus scooted out of the booth and scrambled around tables and chairs to get to the counter. "Maddie, what's that woman's name?"

Maddie just glared at him and said nothing.

"Come on, Maddie! I have to know her name if I'm going to marry her." Marcus clasped his hands under his chin and pursed his lips. "Pretty please? You know her name, don't you?"

"'Course I know her name!" Maddie exclaimed. "How else am I going to know who an order is for?"

"What is it?" Marcus was dancing with excitement. "Tell me, Maddie!"

"Uh-uh," Maddie said, shaking her head. "I'd never do that to the poor girl."

Marcus collapsed on the counter, groaning in frustration. Daniel snorted with laughter back at the booth.

"Maddie, you're killing me," Marcus said. She shook her head in disgust and stomped off to the kitchen, but Marcus didn't mind. It wouldn't be that hard to find out who the new arrival was in this small town.

3

The place Corinne landed on Saturday morning, for her first Ohio adventure, was a tiny beach in Huron. At first glance, the area looked like a simple playground, but once she crossed to the far side of the equipment, she realized the land sloped downward to a quaint shoreline bordered on three sides by the water.

Lake Erie might have been one of the smallest of the Great Lakes, but it certainly looked big enough to Corinne, growing up landlocked as she had. Any lakes in Corinne's experience were of the sort that you could wave to a friend standing on the far shore. Here, the far shore was Canada.

To her left, a couple of children were excavating new riverways in the sand and then constructing dams for the sheer delight of watching the moving water destroy them. To her right, a colony of herring gulls swooped in to partake of any discarded tidbits from visitors' picnic baskets.

Along the front edge of the water was a small breakwall. Corinne walked the entire length of the beach along its huge flat-topped boulders. The breeze was slight enough that the rocks weren't wet and slippery from spray, but it was brisk enough to keep her moving. She pledged to come back in summer when the air and water were warmer and it would be comfortable to relax on the beach, doing nothing more than taking in the gentle sound of water lapping at the shore.

For now, though, Corinne needed to get back to Sutton. She needed to find a church. Over lunch she searched online, only to realize how few choices there were. Not like in the city. When she got in her car to go check them out, it took all of thirty minutes.

The one that caught her eye was a stately brick building situated on the corner of two side streets, across Main and a bit south of her little house. More than a dozen arched stained glass windows adorned both the front of the building and the side next to the parking lot. *Sunday morning worship: 10:30 a.m.* the sign read.

Perfect, Corinne thought. *I'll be there.*

Next morning Corinne parked her car and followed a group of people through the heavy wooden doors of the main entrance.

The low hum of conversations enveloped her. Plush but aged carpet muffled the footfalls of worshippers as they moved about the room. Warm spring sunshine filtered in through the colored glass.

As an usher handed her a bulletin, Corinne slipped into a seat just inside the door. She glanced through the order of worship, then began studying the people. It was easy to do, as the sanctuary was arranged in an arc with four sections of cushioned wooden pews angled toward the front. What she saw was lots of older folks. *Nothing unusual there.* However, she also saw plenty of younger people, too. One such woman, who was sitting with her husband a couple sections over, caught her eye and waved. Corinne returned the gesture, surprised at being noticed. She was more used to blending in among the masses.

At the beginning of the service was a simple, yet heartfelt hymn arrangement played on the shining grand piano positioned at the far side of the platform. Corinne loved everything about worship, and from the moment the music started, she pushed all distractions from her mind and let the familiar strains wash over her.

At the end of the service was the benediction. "And now," the pastor proclaimed, "may the God of peace sanctify you completely. Go forth from this place and share the love of Christ with others that they may come to know Him. Amen."

Corinne had heard many benedictions in her life; she was a dedicated churchgoer, after all, raised in a family of dedicated churchgoers. But for some reason those words swept over her like a torrent. She gripped the back of the pew to steady herself. *What on earth?*

There was no time for contemplation, however. As the new face of the morning, she found herself the object of much attention. The greetings were similar. "Welcome! It's good to have you with us!" Corinne shook every hand and exchanged names with every person, knowing full well she'd never remember them all. She couldn't imagine needing to, if experience was any guide. Still though, she found it pleasant not to be invisible.

Not so many of the younger crowd stopped by, but the woman from earlier headed straight for Corinne, along with her husband. "Hi!" she said, taking her by the hand. "I don't think we've met."

"We haven't," she replied. "It's my first Sunday here. I'm Corinne Edwards." She shook the woman's hand.

"I'm Becky Fleming and this is my husband, Daniel."

"Nice to meet you both." Corinne shook Daniel's hand as well.

"Likewise," he replied and then squinted. "Say, am I crazy or did I see you at Maddie's Diner on Friday? Lunchtime?"

Corinne blinked. "You might have. I picked up an order. I was in the middle of unpacking."

"So you just moved here!" Becky exclaimed. "That's wonderful!" She linked her arm through Corinne's, and they strolled toward the exit. "Do you have family in town?" Daniel followed behind, listening to every word.

Corinne soon learned that Becky was a schoolteacher and Daniel a contractor. They in turn learned that neither job nor family had brought Corinne to town and were fascinated by the idea that she'd moved to Sutton for no discernible reason.

Having to give a reason was new for Corinne. In the city, people always assumed it was for a job, or never even mentioned it. To Daniel and Becky she said, "I'm just exploring the world."

"How do you decide where to go?" Becky wanted to know.

"I don't. I wake up one morning and know it's time to move on. I go, and somehow, I know when I've arrived." She paused as a new thought occurred to her. "It's almost like I've been prompted."

Becky stopped walking and turned toward Corinne. "Have you accepted Jesus as your Savior?"

Startled by the direct question, Corinne answered almost without thinking. "I have. When I was in junior high."

"Well, then," Becky said. "I imagine it's God doing the prompting, don't you?" She relinked her arm through Corinne's, and they walked along a row of parked cars.

Corinne had never considered this before. As far as she knew, there'd been no apparent reason for any of the places she'd lived, other than her own curiosity. "Why would He do that? I mean, what does it matter where I live?"

"Oh, I'm sure it has to do with His call on your life. How do you serve Him?"

"Bec, come on," Daniel broke in. "Go easy on the poor girl."

Corinne, a little taken aback by the woman's directness, was grateful for Daniel's intervention. She was, however, also curious, because there was something about this woman's easy ability to discuss faith that appealed to Corinne. She stopped walking and turned to answer Becky's question with raw honesty. "I don't know if I am."

Daniel studied her for a moment. "You know, God works through each of us uniquely. Some He calls to a very specific purpose, and others He calls to live out their faith in everyday life."

Something clicked in Corinne's mind. "That reminds me of the pastor's final words this morning."

Daniel was quiet, trying to recall the words of the benediction.

"Really, Daniel?" Becky teased. "Were you even listening?"

"All right, smartie. You tell me what he said, if you can remember." Daniel winked at Corinne.

It was such a simple little exchange. One of a million that must pass between husbands and wives every single day. At any other time, with any other people, Corinne might have noted the barb hitting its mark. But not here, not with them. It was obvious they were just having fun together.

After a moment spent savoring the beauty of such a thing, Corinne recollected her thoughts and summarized for them. "The pastor sent us forth to share Christ with others."

"I remember now," Daniel said. "'Go forth from this place,' Pastor Stephen said. You never know when something in your life might touch another person's heart for Christ."

Has anything in my life ever done that? Corinne wondered as they continued walking. Then a more disturbing question arose in her mind. *Have I ever shared Christ with anyone at all?*

There was to be no more discussion about it this day, however, because they had arrived at Corinne's car. "This is me," she said, already hoping for the opportunity to continue the conversation another time.

Becky reached out to give her a farewell hug. "I'm so glad God directed you here, Corinne. See you next Sunday!"

4

On Friday, Marcus and Daniel were back at Maddie's and sitting in their usual booth. The laminate tabletop was worn but clean. A napkin dispenser and small wire basket filled with sugar packets had been pushed up against the wall to make room for paperwork. Over lunch they had reviewed a new contract for a whole house remodeling job Daniel's company had landed.

"Don't get lazy about the draws, Daniel," Marcus advised. "Follow the contract."

"Alrighty, boss." Daniel closed the folder and set it on the seat beside him.

"Now," Marcus said, clicking his pen and dropping it in his briefcase. "What have you heard about this new woman in town?"

"What new woman?" Daniel raised his eyebrows innocently.

"Don't be an ass."

Daniel smirked. "I thought you were going to find her."

"Not getting a whole lot of cooperation from the townsfolk. I called Bernie, just to see if he'd rented to anyone new and all he would say was, 'That's confidential, man. That's confidential!'" Marcus snorted and grabbed his glass. He downed the iced tea and wiped his lips.

"Well, you could always stake out the grocery store. I'm sure she's got to shop sometime."

Marcus gave his friend a withering look. "Have you heard anything or not?"

Daniel just shrugged and looked away.

"Oh my god. You have!" He peered at him across the table. "Spill it, Daniel."

Daniel sighed in defeat. "We met her at church on Sunday."

Marcus leaned back in his seat. "A church girl. How about that." He mused over this piece of news for a bit and then looked back at Daniel. "And?"

"And what?"

"What else did you learn about her?"

"Just her name, and that she definitely moved here. That's about it."

"So, what's her name?"

"Uh-uh," Daniel said. "I'm not telling you that."

"What?" Marcus threw out his hands. "Why not?"

Daniel looked his friend straight in the eye. "If you want to know her name, you're going to have to come to church."

Marcus scowled at him, but Daniel was resolute. "You say you want to meet her, now you know where to find her."

He couldn't argue with that. Truth was, he'd been dodging Daniel's invitations to church for years, but this was too good to pass up. Besides, what could it hurt?

"Fine. What time's the service?"

Sunday morning Marcus whistled tunelessly as he showered and shaved and anticipated the meeting to come. He almost felt like a kid waiting to open presents on Christmas morning. He'd met plenty of women in his time, but he'd never done it quite like this before.

After drying off he went to the closet and pulled open the doors. It was half empty. *Sure wouldn't mind sharing this space*, he thought, then immediately added out loud, "Let's not get ahead of ourselves."

He selected a suit coat and tie, something he seldom did even for his law practice, and dressed quickly. Then he grabbed a brush and tried to make sense of the unruly waves of jet-black hair that always fell back across his forehead no matter what. Giving it up as a lost cause, he headed down the open staircase and out the door, not even stopping for breakfast.

A dozen vehicles were already in the lot, but none of them belonged to his friends. He leaned against his car, enjoying the breeze as he waited for them to arrive. In spite of his own warning, his thoughts were consumed with the possibilities that awaited him once he walked through those doors. Possibilities that had nothing to do with God.

Daniel and Becky arrived, and once they were inside and seated, Marcus began looking around, trying to catch a glimpse of the girl. Nothing. *She better show up*, he thought, and contemplated what he'd do if she didn't.

Suddenly, there she was. Becky motioned her over and the young woman slid in beside her. Daniel leaned forward to say hello, but before he could make any introductions, the service began.

Marcus played it cool, feigning attention to the events up front, but stealing a glimpse of her every so often. She was completely focused on the service. He didn't think she'd even noticed him. Yet.

It was interminable, the wait. *Please God, let her be worth it.* Marcus scoffed at himself. *A prayer? Where did that come from?* He cleared his throat and shifted in his seat. Daniel leaned over and whispered, "Stop fidgeting or I'm going to put you in time out when we get home."

"Shut up," Marcus whispered back.

When it was over, everybody stood for one last word from the pastor, and then Marcus nudged Daniel in the ribs. "Dude."

"I know, I know," Daniel said. "Let's get out of the pew." He pushed Marcus toward the aisle and beckoned his wife and Corinne to follow.

"Corinne," Daniel said. "I'd like to introduce my friend and legal counsel, Marcus Hunter. Marcus, this is Corinne Edwards."

"Hello, Corinne."

"Hi," she replied, shaking his proffered hand.

Corinne pulled her hand away, but he didn't let go. She blinked in surprise. Marcus grinned and then let go.

"Hey, Corinne, I want to introduce—" Becky started to say, at the exact same time that Marcus said,

"Daniel here tells me you've just moved to town."

Now Corinne raised an eyebrow. "Did he?" She turned to stare at Daniel.

He looked embarrassed. "Uh, yeah. It came up."

Without missing a beat Marcus continued. "You move here on purpose?"

Corinne jerked her head back toward him. "Why? Doesn't anybody move to Sutton on purpose?"

"Oh sure. It's a good place. But seriously, what brings you here?"

"Nothing in particular."

Marcus squinted at her. "That's a cryptic answer. Where are you from?"

Corinne smirked. "That's an ambiguous question."

"It's a simple question!" Marcus countered.

Daniel guffawed but Corinne didn't waiver. She pierced Marcus with a steady gaze. For a moment, he lost his train of thought. All that registered were her dark eyes, challenging, and yet playful. His pulse quickened.

"Fair enough," he found himself saying. "How about this: prior to arriving in Sutton, what was your city and state of residence?"

At that question, Corinne's face lit up. "Phoenix, Arizona."

Becky squeaked in surprise. "Are you serious?" Corinne turned to her and nodded, but Marcus still kept going.

"Now we're getting somewhere. Is Phoenix your hometown?"

"No."

"And what city do you call home?"

"Indianapolis."

Marcus thought for a second. "What took you to Phoenix?"

Corinne pursed her lips and looked skyward before answering. "Nothing in particular."

Marcus laughed outright. "The plot thickens." He tilted his head. "You're not running from the law are you, because I know a good lawyer."

"Pfft." Corinne rolled her eyes.

"So, Indianapolis to Phoenix to Sutton." Marcus crossed his arms over his chest and stroked his chin. "Huh."

"Well," Corinne said. "Not quite." Now it was Marcus's turn to be surprised, and Daniel hooted. Corinne chuckled at both of them and wrinkled her nose at Becky.

Holy crap, Marcus thought. For a moment he stood motionless, staring at the woman in front of him. She was enjoying this as much as he was! He rallied his senses and said, "There's more? I'd very much like to hear about that. How about over lunch?"

"Oh, for heaven's sake, Marcus," Becky exclaimed. She hooked her arm through Corinne's. "We're going to go meet some other people." She turned to Corinne. "That okay with you?"

"Absolutely." To Marcus Corinne said, "Thanks, anyway," and turned her back on him.

Marcus watched as the two women walked away. Before they were out of earshot he called after them, "It was a pleasure to meet you, Corinne."

Corinne lifted her hand in slight acknowledgment.

Apparently, God did answer prayers. Who knew?

Daniel turned to Marcus. "Sorry, big guy. Total strikeout. I told you she wasn't your type."

Marcus scowled. "What are you talking about?"

"She turned you down flat."

"Maybe so, but that was most definitely not a strikeout." He clapped Daniel on the back. "You've been out of the game too long, my man."

"Yeah well, you need to get out and stay out."

"I'm working on it," Marcus replied, looking up just in time to see Corinne disappear into the crowd. *Definitely working on it.*

5

Corinne excused herself from Becky before they reached the group of women and fled from the church. She unlocked the car, threw her purse on the passenger side, and climbed in. She stuck the key in the ignition, and then stopped. Her hands fell to her lap, and she collapsed against the seat. *What just happened?* She stared out the window as she reviewed the scene in her mind, laughed to herself, and then frowned.

She started the car and drove out of the lot. A few minutes later she pulled in her driveway and went inside. She changed clothes, got lunch, and threw a load of laundry in the wash, all on auto pilot. Her mind was still on the encounter.

The Encounter. Good name for it. Oh, she couldn't deny she'd enjoyed the banter, but what the heck was that? He "told him"? Had they been talking about her?

Part of her was gratified, because she also couldn't deny that she'd found him attractive. But the other part of her was a bit shocked by his brazenness. *Not sure that's what I'm looking for,* she thought, and then chided herself for even contemplating such an idea after a whole two-minute conversation. If she had learned anything about relationships over the past decade, it was not to rush in.

Determined not to let any old memories—or even these new ones, for that matter—overshadow her Sunday afternoon, she brushed it all aside and decided to check out the local park. Corinne had always enjoyed spending time in the parks wherever she lived. This one was just a few blocks from her house, so she walked. Upon arriving, however, she found it deserted. Even the playground equipment was uninhabited. Corinne looked around for a sign, wondering if it was closed. *Nothing.* In the city, there were always people in the parks. She was confused. *Where do people hang out around here?*

She was tempted to turn around and go home; somehow it wasn't the same without people. This thought surprised her because she seldom interacted with anyone while she was there anyway.

But Corinne wasn't one to give up quite so easily. Besides, this was why she was here, to explore and experience and enjoy. She'd done plenty of it on her own. Who cared if no one else was around?

For such a small park, it had several nice walking trails that wound through the woods surrounding it. She took them all, and although they weren't challenging, they were pleasant enough. Afterward, she took a foray onto the swings. *Why not? Nobody else is using them.* Then she sprawled out on the grass and read her book. All in all, it was a decent afternoon, even if not quite what she had expected.

Later when Corinne returned home and was finishing her laundry for the week, her thoughts returned to the events of the morning. She had looked forward to another conversation with Daniel and Becky about matters of faith. It hadn't happened. She could have kicked herself for walking out like that, and yet it felt like the right thing to do. At least it's what she'd felt prompted to do.

Corinne paused in the middle of folding a towel. *"I imagine it's God doing the prompting, don't you?"* Becky's words echoed in her brain. *Was she right? Did He prompt me today, too? And if He had, why?* Corinne had no idea.

As she crawled into bed that night, she found herself wondering what Becky would think. She wondered if her departure had seemed rude to the woman. Then she started worrying that Daniel and Becky might have taken offense and would no longer be interested in any further conversations with her.

"Oh, God!" Corinne exclaimed. "Please don't let me have screwed that up!"

It wasn't the most auspicious of starts to her prayers, but it was heartfelt. She continued, lifting it all to God, and then ended with this earnest plea. "God please let me have an opportunity to make things right with Becky. Amen."

At the end of her workday on Monday, Corinne was glad to shut down her bookkeeping software and fire up a video chat with Evelyn instead. Evelyn was the Sunday School teacher who had shared the gospel with her and been her mentor ever since. Corinne told her everything that had taken place since her move to Sutton.

"Have you prayed about all of this?" Evelyn asked.

"Sort of," Corinne replied.

"Okay," Evelyn said. "Maybe you can work toward being more purposeful about that. God's role is to guide you. Yours is to be obedient when He does, but He wants to hear from you, too."

Corinne thought yet again of Becky's words. "Do you think it could be God prompting me all those times?"

"What do you think?"

"I think yes, but I don't understand why."

"You may never understand. That's part of faith, trusting God enough to obey even when we don't."

Corinne mulled this over. "It's not like I made a conscious choice to obey. I didn't even comprehend that it might be God prompting me."

Evelyn's eyes were serious and thoughtful. "Now that you're aware, it would be wise to talk to Him about it. Thank Him, first of all, for working in your life. Then seek discernment for His presence and ask for His protection from anything that might try to mislead you. Last of all, ask Him to guide you toward more purposeful obedience."

Corinne began to feel the weight of the charge set before her. These were not concrete tasks to be checked off a list like she did daily for her clients. These were big picture items played out in the snapshots of daily life.

"So basically, I need to stick close to God in prayer."

"Yes," Evelyn said. "That's always a good idea."

"What about sharing Christ with others? I haven't been able to get those words out of my mind since that first Sunday in church here. I'm just not sure how to do it."

"We often think in terms of doing something big for God," Evelyn said. "But it is often in choosing to behave differently than the rest of the world, in the everyday circumstances of life, that makes people sit up and take notice. Not that appearing different is our goal, but rather that we are so focused on our obedience to God, particularly when it goes against our own will, that it stands out. That is what shows the power of Christ to transform lives."

Corinne was taking it all in but didn't say anything.

"God brings these things to us in His perfect timing, and we can trust Him to provide what we need to serve Him. Keep praying, Corinne, and watch for the ways He leads you to do His will."

Corinne was nothing if not diligent. When she set her mind to a task, she gave it her all. It was the same with this new addition to her prayers. She wasn't sure what she expected to come from them, however, so she was astonished when a mere two days later she went to the grocery store, rounded the end of an aisle, and almost ran smack dab into Becky. Both women were startled by the near collision, but Becky recovered first. "Corinne! I'm so glad to see you!"

"Me too!"

"We didn't have a chance to talk Sunday," Becky said. "And then that introduction happened, and...oh, Corinne! Daniel wasn't gossiping about you! It's just that Marcus asked. We've been praying ever since for a chance to explain."

For a moment, Corinne just stared. *Could she have heard that right?*

Becky continued. "I know Daniel's not here, but on his behalf, if we offended you, we are so sorry." Becky touched her on the arm as she made this earnest plea. "Will you forgive us?"

Corinne's mouth dropped open, but she couldn't say a word. *They were worried about what she thought of them?*

As the seconds ticked by, she saw the light in Becky's eyes falter, and her senses returned. "Oh Becky, of course, but honestly there's nothing to forgive. I'm the one who needs to apologize."

"What for?"

"For running out of church like that. It was rude. I'm sorry."

"It's okay," Becky said, but Corinne could see the confusion on her face, so she explained.

"It was one of those times where I felt like it's what I was supposed to do. Although it seems kind of silly..." Corinne shook her head.

Becky's whole face lit up when she smiled. "All good. And not silly at all! Who am I to stand in the way of God's prompting?"

"If that's even what it was." Corinne was still trying to wrap her head around this idea.

Both women were silent for a moment, pondering. Becky was the first to speak. "It probably was for the best, now that I think about it."

Now it was Corinne's turn to be curious. "How so?"

"Marcus is a great guy, he really is," Becky explained. "But he loves to banter, and sometimes he gets a little intense. He probably would have kept on going had the four of us come back together." She wrinkled her nose. "Not sure how that would have gone."

"No, me either," Corinne said. "Although it wasn't the banter that bothered me. I enjoy that kind of thing." She exhaled through her nose and shook her head. "It was the lunch invitation! It was a little—" She stopped, unable to find the words to explain further, but Becky seemed to understand.

"Oh, I know." Becky rolled her eyes. "Did he seriously expect you to fall into his arms and go to lunch with him? I do not understand what men think sometimes!"

Corinne was surprised—and delighted—with Becky's response. Relieved too. "Thank you."

The two women hugged, and when Becky pulled back, she looked up at Corinne. "You know, if you enjoyed that conversation with Marcus, up until his invitation anyway," here she rolled her eyes again, "then maybe it's a good thing you two met." She winked at Corinne.

Embarrassment caused Corinne's face to grow warm. "I don't know." Then she turned serious. "It's just that you and your husband and I had such a good conversation that first Sunday. I was hoping for the opportunity to have more of those, and I was afraid you wouldn't want to after that little episode."

Becky's eyes softened and she squeezed Corinne's hand. "I do want to, and I have no doubt we'll have lots of opportunities." She pulled away and looked Corinne in the eyes. "There was something about you that very first Sunday that made me come right over after the service." She shook her head. "It seems to me like God is at work in both of our lives."

Corinne could feel the tears forming behind her eyes. She didn't want them to spill over, but it couldn't be helped. Becky offered her a tissue and said, "We've had a spectacular start, haven't we? And because we don't know each other very well yet, we're a little bit uncertain. But that will change over time."

"I hope so. I would love that." Corinne was surprised by how much she meant it. She sniffled and used the tissue to give her nose a gentle blow. After wiping away the last of her renegade tears, she said, "You know, I would have called you about all this, but I didn't know your number."

"Well, let's fix that right now!" Becky pulled out her phone. "Then we'll always be able to reach out to each other, whenever we want to."

"Perfect."

Corinne was at peace once again and satisfied with the outcome. She could not have imagined it getting any better. At least, not until Becky spoke up again.

"Say, next Sunday is a potluck dinner at church. We'd like to have you come as our guest. What do you say?"

"I'd love to!"

6

All week long, whether at work or at play, Marcus could not stop celebrating. Whatever it was that had attracted him to Corinne that day in the diner was borne out in their first—albeit brief—conversation.

Here was a woman who not only engaged his eyes but also his brain. What a welcome change that was! For whatever reason, the type of women Marcus usually met didn't enjoy his banter. In fact, some of them got mad. They just didn't get it. But Corinne did.

Of course, he'd need to make sure it wasn't a fluke; their conversation had been short, after all. And she had walked away. That wasn't a bad thing, per se. If she'd said yes—well, that would have been too easy.

Unless walking away meant that she was offended. Or dating someone. *Hmm.* Well, he'd just need to see her again to figure it out. The downside of it all was that he had no way to do so except another church service. But that hadn't been a big deal after all, and besides, he intended to develop other options real soon.

Next Sunday morning found him sitting in the same spot next to Daniel, staring at the wooden doors. The service was just about to start, and Marcus leaned forward to speak to Becky. "Where's your friend?"

"Oh, she'll be here. I told her about the dinner and invited her to be our guest."

"Wait. You talked to her this week?"

"Uh-huh. I ran into her at the grocery store."

Daniel smirked. "Told ya," he whispered. "You could have staked out the store."

"Shut up," Marcus whispered back.

The music began and Marcus considered leaving. But then what? He was not going to sit at the grocery store. He wasn't a stalker, for God's sake. He was still mulling this over a few minutes later when the door opened, and

Corinne slipped inside. She took a seat at the very back of the nearest section and then looked over at them. Becky waved and motioned for her to come sit with them, but she shook her head. Leaning back in her seat, she took a deep breath and blew it out. Then she rubbed her face with her hands and ran her fingers through her hair.

Those two mundane actions took Marcus by surprise. Did women do that? Somehow, the idea of it appealed to him, and he was mesmerized once again. He watched her as much as he dared throughout the hour and spent the balance of his time anticipating their next conversation. To everything else, he was oblivious.

As soon as the service ended, he stepped out of the pew and headed straight for her. She was gathering up her purse when he said, "Good morning, Corinne."

She glanced up. "Good morning."

Marcus tapped his wrist. "You were late."

"I was," she said and turned toward him.

"Why?"

Corinne raised an eyebrow. "Why are you asking?"

"Just want to know."

Corinne bobbed her head. "Mmm," was all she said.

When the silence lengthened, Marcus realized she wasn't going to answer. He didn't want to blow up this conversation too, if that's what happened last time, so he scrambled for what to say next. What ended up coming out of his mouth was, "Sorry."

"For what?" she asked. Her gaze was inscrutable.

Marcus's mouth dropped open, but no words came out. He couldn't tell if she was playing with him or being serious. *Better to err on the side of caution.* "I was trying to be...I don't know, playful, I guess. Instead, I ended up being rude. I didn't mean to be."

To his surprise, her features softened. "I forgive you." That's all she said.

Marcus's insides quivered at the words. He stared at her uncomprehendingly, and so she spoke again. "We all do stuff like that sometimes, right? And we all need forgiveness." Her eyes were warm now, and she just looked so—friendly. It sounded silly, but Marcus thought he had never seen anything so beautiful in his life.

Truly beautiful because in his experience, women didn't forgive. "Thank you," was all he could say.

"Of course." Corinne made no move to leave the pew, but rather looked around the sanctuary, taking it in as if for the very first time.

"But was everything okay this morning?" Marcus still wanted to know the answer to this question.

Corinne turned back to him. "Oh, yeah. I just had a flat tire."

"Ooh, not fun. Did you change it?"

"Ah, no. I wouldn't even be able to get the lug nuts off. I walked."

Marcus swept his gaze over her, noting the slacks and blouse and comfortable shoes. "Well, I guess you were dressed right for it."

Corinne looked amused. "I changed."

Marcus was embarrassed. "I'm doing just great here, aren't I?"

Corinne waved it away. "You're fine." Her eyes twinkled.

"Corinne!" This was Becky. She and Daniel had made their way across the sanctuary, and she rushed up to give her a hug. "Hey, girl!"

Marcus turned to Daniel. "Corinne had a flat tire this morning."

"Oh!" Becky interrupted, holding her at arm's length. "Is that why you came in late?" Corinne nodded.

Marcus continued. "You want to help me change that this afternoon?"

"Sure," Daniel replied. "I'd be happy to."

Marcus turned back to Corinne. "You've got a spare, right?"

Corinne stared at him for a second. "Are you serious?"

"Of course."

"That would be fantastic. Yeah, I've got a spare."

"Okay, then. Consider it done."

"Wow." She looked shocked. "Thank you."

"You're welcome."

His offer had come naturally, and almost without thought. But the fact that it put him back in Corinne's good graces was a welcome bonus. Two brief conversations were all they'd had, yet already Marcus knew that she did not operate like most women of his acquaintance. He found this enticing, and he wanted to know more.

"You should've called," Becky spoke up again. "We would've picked you up."

"Oh!" Corinne exclaimed, startled back to reality. "I didn't even think of that."

"How far did you walk?" Becky wanted to know.

"Eight blocks."

"Well, thank goodness you weren't wearing heels!"

Marcus saw the delight envelope Corinne's face. She looked at Becky with what he could only describe as fondness, a smile forming on her lips. "That is a good thing," she replied.

"Let's go get some dinner and then we'll change that tire," Daniel said.

"Sounds good," Becky replied. They headed across the sanctuary toward fellowship hall. Marcus and Corinne fell into step behind them.

"I'm curious that you did walk," Marcus ventured to say. "Seems like a flat tire would have been a good reason to stay home."

Corinne drew in a breath as she thought. "It might be for some things, I suppose, but not this." She gestured around the room. "Worshiping together with other believers is important to me."

Marcus tipped his head in acknowledgement but said nothing. It wasn't familiar territory for him.

"Where do you want to sit?" Daniel asked as they entered the hall.

"I see four over there," Becky said, pointing. "Let's grab them."

As they secured their seats, Daniel asked, "What would you ladies like to drink?"

"I'll take water," Corinne said.

"Lemonade for me," added Becky.

"Coming right up. Marcus, give me a hand?" The girls settled into seats next to each other and chatted while the guys got drinks and the room filled with people.

An older man came alongside Daniel and clapped him on the shoulder. "Good to see you, Daniel. How's life treating you?"

"Hey, Roger. Real good. How was your vacation?"

"Oh, it was great. But it's always good to get back to worship with my church family. Who's your friend here?"

Daniel introduced the two men, and they shook hands. "It's a pleasure to meet you, Marcus, and a real pleasure to see you in worship this morning."

"Thank you, sir," Marcus replied, taken aback. "Nice to meet you, too."

Soon the pastor called for everyone's attention and offered a prayer for the meal. Before long they each had a massive load of potluck goodies on their plates, and they settled in to enjoy the meal.

"I don't think I've ever seen so much food!" Marcus exclaimed.

"Every fifth Sunday," Becky said.

"Seriously?" Corinne asked. "That's awesome. I love potlucks."

"I'm a fan," Marcus declared and dug in. The four ate in silence for a couple of minutes until the sharpest pangs of hunger subsided, and then they chatted amongst themselves. Eventually talk turned to Corinne and her recent move. "I'd love to know more about the 'in-between Indianapolis and Phoenix' part," Marcus said, "if you're willing to share."

"Sure." Corinne hastened to swallow her bite of cheesy potatoes.

"So, where'd you live before Arizona?"

"I was in Colorado and before that, Philadelphia."

"Oh, wow," Becky said. "Big moves!"

"Yes, but worth it. Lots of cool stuff to see everywhere I've been." She snagged a forkful of broccoli rice casserole.

Marcus chewed on a bite of homemade dinner roll as he took it all in. Then he asked, "Is there more?"

Corinne set down her fork and ticked the cities off on her fingers. "Before Philly, I was in New York State. Chicago was before that. The first place I went to was Nashville, shortly after I graduated college. I spent just about a year in each place."

"You change jobs every time you move?" Daniel wanted to know.

"Oh no. I carry my business with me."

"What business?" Marcus asked.

"Accounting. I started doing contract bookkeeping work for a businessman from my home church while I was still in school. He gave me several referrals, and by the time I graduated, I already had a real decent client base. I realized I liked the freedom of what I was doing and how I was doing it." She shrugged. "So I kept on."

With the meal all but forgotten, Corinne continued her story. "I spent the summer marketing and expanding. In the fall I signed my first subcontractor and then celebrated by taking a vacation—to Nashville."

She let the memory wash over her. "I was going to spend a week sightseeing but also keep up with work." She made a face. "I soon realized that wasn't feasible."

She glanced around at her rapt audience. "So, I stayed. Did my sightseeing on the evenings and weekends. That's what I've done ever since, everywhere I've lived."

"Wow," Becky said, and they all fell silent.

Corinne was the first to emerge from her reverie. She drained her cup and pushed back from the table, but Marcus held out his hand. "Allow me. Water, right?"

"Oh! Yes, thank you."

As he threaded his way among the tables toward the drinks, he contemplated her story. A unique history, no doubt about that. But not flighty; she was a businesswoman after all, in finance and with a college degree. That had to mean something.

If she'd chosen to live a nomadic lifestyle, where was the harm in that? Surely she was level-headed enough that she'd be glad to settle down in one place once she fell in love. The very thought made Marcus short of breath.

Roger was refilling drink cups as Marcus approached. "Enjoying the meal, son?" he asked.

"Yeah, the food is great!" Marcus said, relieved to be distracted from his thoughts. "I think I've eaten too much already."

"It is an occupational hazard of church potluck dinners." He stood aside as Marcus filled the water cup. "That young lady over there. Friend of yours?"

Marcus looked up. "Oh, no," he said, knowing what Roger meant. "She just moved here." He picked up the cup and glanced over at Corinne. She and Becky were chattering away. He turned back to Roger. "I think she and Becky have hit it off already."

"That's wonderful," Roger said. "God sure is good to bring just the right people into our lives, at just the right time." He smiled at Marcus. "I'll let you get back to your friends."

Marcus frowned. Corinne showing up in Sutton was random; she said so herself. Nobody orchestrated it. Brushing the comment aside, he returned and placed the cup on the table, then sat down.

"Thank you," Corinne said.

"You're welcome."

After the dinner, Corinne and Becky gathered up plates and dishes while the men helped put away chairs. Out in the parking lot, Marcus said, "Corinne, you can ride with me. Daniel, you guys follow, and we'll get that tire changed."

"Sounds good," Daniel said, and he and Becky headed for their car.

Corinne opened her mouth to speak and then closed it again. Marcus raised his eyebrows. "Is that okay?"

She looked embarrassed. "I guess it would be kind of silly to walk, wouldn't it?"

"It kind of would." Marcus looked at her solemnly. "Plus, I'd have to drive very slowly to follow you."

Corinne tipped her head and gave him a look. "Okay then." Marcus's eyes twinkled as he held open the passenger side door for her.

After she'd given him the address, she said, "Thanks again for doing this. It's really nice of you guys."

"Sure." He looked sideways at her. "Don't people help each other in all those places you've lived?"

She hesitated in answering. "I'm sure they do. I guess I've always just taken care of things myself."

"Nothing wrong with that."

Corinne looked out the window. Then she said, "No, I suppose not."

Marcus's curiosity was piqued, but those eight blocks had gone fast, and Corinne was already saying, "Here we are."

He turned into the driveway. "Oh yeah. That's definitely flat." Corinne groaned and removed the car key from her ring to hand to him.

Becky got out of their car exclaiming, "Oh! You live in the dollhouse!"

Corinne gave her an inquisitive look. "Is that what it's called?"

"That's what I call it. It's adorable!"

"Well, come on inside and I'll give you the grand tour." She turned to Marcus. "You guys need anything else?"

He shook his head. "We'll be fine."

Corinne and Becky disappeared inside the house, and Marcus and Daniel got busy changing the tire. "Well?" Daniel asked. Marcus just grinned.

When the women came back outside, they were carrying glasses of iced tea. The guys were loading the damaged tire in the trunk and putting away the jack. Corinne handed each of them a glass. "Thank you so much for doing this. It'll make it easier to deal with this week."

"You're welcome," Daniel replied.

"Anytime," Marcus added. They leaned against the cars, sipping iced tea as they chatted. After a bit Marcus looked toward the house and around the postage stamp yard and said, "You need some chairs out here."

Corinne followed his gaze. "Yeah maybe. But..."

"But...what?" Marcus prompted.

"I try to keep my possessions light. Makes it easier when the time comes to move."

"Oh, Corinne," Becky exclaimed. "You can't be thinking of moving again already! You just got here!"

"I'm not, I swear! I was just answering the question." Corinne went on to explain. "I've learned moving's a whole lot easier—and more fun—when you don't have so much stuff to deal with."

"I cannot imagine moving every year," Becky mused. "Isn't it hard to leave behind everybody you've met?"

Corinne looked uncertain. "It can be, I suppose." After a moment she continued. "But honestly people come and go so much that circles are always changing anyway. You know what I mean?"

Becky shook her head slowly. "I don't think that's how things are here, but maybe that's just because we've lived in one place for so long." She pursed her lips and squinted at Corinne. "You know what I think? You've been in big cities for too long. We need to get you properly introduced to small town life, that's all."

Daniel sucked in his breath. "Corinne, you are in for it now!"

"You hush up!" Becky punched him playfully in the arm.

"Yeah, Daniel, hush up! Let Becky work her magic." Marcus winked at Corinne, and she blushed in spite of herself.

During his drive home a short time later, however, Marcus's thoughts grew serious once again. *Why did Corinne move so much? Was it just for fun, or was it something else? And what was her relationship status? Did that have anything to do with it?*

Marcus shook his head to clear it of the questions he had no answers for. He had to believe she wanted to settle down eventually. It's what everybody wanted, wasn't it? It's what he wanted, even though he sucked at it. He sighed as he pulled into his driveway a few minutes later. There was a lot he didn't know about this woman, but one thing he was sure of. He wanted to learn more.

He went into the house and dropped his keys on the table. He just hoped his interest in her wouldn't come back to bite him. After living in so many different places, and with such a philosophy, could Corinne truly be content to settle in a small town like Sutton, Ohio? From everything she'd said, Marcus knew he had one year to convince her that she would.

7

Corinne was not at all certain she agreed with Becky's assessment of things. In her experience people were the same no matter where you lived: busy and self-absorbed. It's not that they were unfriendly; they just weren't available. Didn't have the bandwidth to add anything—or anyone—new. It's how Corinne had come to be so independent over the years of her travels. It was easier to manage things herself than to try to depend on someone else.

Although these people, Daniel and Becky and Marcus, didn't fit that mold. They had just helped her with her car, and she hadn't even asked them to. They had given up their time and gotten their hands dirty. She was grateful.

But there were still the challenges of small-town living. No matter how charming it was, or how helpful the people, there was simply nothing to do. All her excursions so far had been somewhere else, except for the park. The empty park. By living here, she'd resigned herself to driving farther than ever to do her sightseeing.

Still though. She found herself drawn to Daniel and Becky. And Marcus, too. Could the pleasure of these developing relationships be worth the inconvenience of more driving? *Hmm.*

Corinne washed up the glasses after carrying them into the house and then completed her usual Sunday chores. Her phone said it was 3:00. Too early to be done for the day; too late to head out of town. The park was probably dead. Corinne pursed her lips to one side. She hadn't planned anything today because of the potluck. Now she was stuck with nothing to do.

Why here, God? I don't know what to do with myself. I can't hang out with friends all the time. If He had directed her here, as Becky surmised, what was the reason?

Unable to come up with any better solution, she grabbed a book and headed out the front door to sit on the step.

The house she had rented was tiny, just four rooms, but it had a concrete slab along the entire front which served as a porch. It was not a huge area, but it was enough to hold a couple of deck chairs. Corinne snorted. Marcus wasn't exactly subtle. Maybe he had an ulterior motive in helping her with her car. *Although it seemed legit. Just like when he filled my water cup.* If it was legit, it was refreshing. If it was just a way to spend more time with her, at least it was an interesting approach.

Corinne pushed those thoughts from her mind. He was getting in her head, and attracted or not, it was too soon to let him be there. She barely knew him, after all. *Not that it necessarily made a difference how long you knew a person.* Corinne groaned as that thought dredged up unwelcome memories from college.

Shortly before graduation, she and her boyfriend had started talking about marriage. Just talking, but before they'd made any decisions, he started issuing directives for her career path. Directives that became more demanding and less friendly as time went on. Things like, where she could apply for jobs and how long she would work there before quitting to raise their family.

It wasn't that she had anything against raising a family. It's that he assumed he got to make all these decisions on his own without any input from her. And they weren't even engaged!

Corinne was glad he had shown his true colors before they made anything permanent. The thing that shook her up, though, was that even though they'd been dating for an entire year, in all that time she'd never seen any indication that he was anything but a nice Christian guy.

She had never since been able to decide if she had been blind to it or if he was just good at hiding it. Either way, it left her a little gun-shy about trusting people. Guys, specifically.

So yeah, it was too soon to let Marcus into her head.

Corinne took a deep breath and then blew it all away. She picked up her book and started to read. It was a good distraction, but it didn't last long. Soon her back started to ache from hunching over. She had to concede that a deck chair would be nice.

Two would be better.

A self-conscious titter bubbled forth. The unbidden thought was funny and did more to lighten her mood than the book had. Truth was, she did like Marcus's style. He made her laugh. She just had to be careful.

She closed her book again and this time laid it on her lap. Hearing shouts and squeals from down the street, she turned and saw a group of children playing together in a front yard. *So that's where they hang out.*

As she contemplated this place where she had landed and how different it was from anything she had ever known, she had to acknowledge there were things she liked about it. The sound of those children's voices was one of them. Less traffic was another. And of course, the people.

Perhaps it would take a little more effort to figure out how to thrive in these circumstances. Perhaps it would be worth it. She could stand to do a little more driving. She'd just have to plan ahead and allow extra time. No big deal. She could have a successful year of sightseeing in Ohio, even from Sutton.

As she crawled into bed that night, she thought back to Evelyn's recommendation to pray over the circumstance with Daniel and Becky. That had worked very well, so she figured she'd try it with this situation, too.

"Dear God," she prayed. "Help me to keep my eyes fixed on the goal and not be distracted by whatever is going on around me. And help me to be careful, no matter how enticing something might be." She stopped and then almost grudgingly added, "Or someone. Amen."

On Friday a curious thing happened. Corinne snapped her computer shut promptly at 5:00, threw some clothes in a bag, and jumped in the car. Within minutes she was out of town and headed south toward Cincinnati. She hadn't planned to do an overnight trip this weekend; she simply felt compelled to do so.

8

So, it wasn't a fluke, that first conversation with Corinne. His second meeting with her, whatever little conversations they'd had, convinced him of that. She was intelligent and quick thinking and knew her own mind. What wasn't to love? Or like, anyway, he was quick to correct himself.

Plus, after thinking it over all week, he felt pretty certain he could convince her to want to stick around.

The only thing was this deal about church. She was way into it. To be sure, Daniel had bugged him for years to join him and Becky in attending, but other than that, Daniel didn't say much about it. It was a nonissue with his friends, so Marcus assumed it would end up the same way with Corinne.

Having made up his mind—and knowing the clock was ticking—Marcus didn't waste any time. On Friday he took more care in dressing for work. A button-down shirt instead of a polo. Slacks, instead of blue jeans. He started out the day freshly shaven but couldn't help where that ended up by five pm.

His intention was to stop by Corinne's house right after work to see if she was up for dinner that evening. An on-the-spot invitation should do the trick. Especially since he hadn't thought to get her phone number last Sunday. Either he was losing his touch or…

Or she was turning his brain to jelly. He waved both of those thoughts away. He'd get back on track once they were dating.

At the last minute on Friday, however, he got caught on a phone call that carried him well past quitting time. By the time he finished, his secretary had gone, leaving him to turn off lights and lock up.

Thus, it was nearly 6:00 by the time he pulled up in front of Corinne's little house, only to find it dark and empty and her car gone. He slumped in his seat. He had assumed she'd be around on Friday evening, even if she was gone all day Saturday.

No matter: he'd try again tomorrow.

Sunday morning found Marcus up early and getting ready for church, despite his best efforts not to need to. Corinne hadn't been around Saturday either, so his goal for the weekend had been shot. He thought he'd at least try to salvage it with Sunday lunch.

Marcus ran his fingers through his hair. The dark waves fell right back across his forehead as they always did, so he gave it up and headed out the door.

He was running early, but still found people gathered and chatting in small groups. He recognized Roger when the older man approached. "Good morning, Marcus! Beautiful day, isn't it?" The two men shook hands.

"I guess so. How are you, Roger?"

"I'm doing very well, thank you. The Lord has seen fit to allow me to wake up this morning and to live in a country where I can worship Him freely. I have no complaints."

Marcus raised his eyebrows. Such thoughts had never occurred to him.

"So, tell me, what do you do for a living?" Roger wanted to know.

"I'm an attorney."

"What field?"

"Pretty typical mix for a small-town practice. Estate planning, contracts, family law. Lots of divorce cases."

"Ah yes," Roger mused. "It must be heartbreaking to have so many of those."

Marcus shrugged. "Eh, it keeps the bills paid."

Roger studied his face for a moment. "I imagine it does." Then he clapped him on the shoulder and said, "It's good to see you here this morning, son." And with that, he moved off to greet more new arrivals.

Marcus could not say why this conversation left him dissatisfied. Perhaps it was just one more thing that didn't go as expected this weekend. He was deep in thought about this when he realized Corinne was through the door and headed in his direction.

"Morning, Marcus."

"Hello there. Heels today, I see. No more flat tires?"

"All tires are fully functional, thank goodness. How are you?"

Marcus pondered the question a moment. "I'm doing all right." Corinne tipped her head, curiosity touching her brow, but she said nothing. Marcus gestured toward the pew. "Shall we sit?" Corinne took a seat toward the middle of the pew and Marcus slid in after her.

"How's the sightseeing?"

Corinne looked up in surprise and then a smile spread across her face. "It's going well."

"What'd you do this weekend?" She told him about her trip south to the Creation Museum.

"That's a lot of driving for a day trip."

"Oh, I left Friday evening. It gave me more time at the museum but still got me home in time for church."

Church again. Wow. Out loud he said, "Oh, I see. An overnight trip. You do that a lot?"

Before she could answer, Daniel and Becky arrived, and much to Marcus's chagrin, Becky commandeered Corinne's attention for the last few minutes before the service began. Daniel just raised a hand in greeting from down the row. *No matter,* Marcus thought. He'd ask her to lunch, for real this time, after the service. At least he was sitting by her today. That was a step in the right direction.

As the music started, Marcus found his thoughts returning to the conversation with Roger. He still couldn't figure out why it bothered him so much. And then of course there was Corinne and church. She arranged her weekend schedule so she could be here this morning. He hoped it wasn't going to be more of an issue than he'd bargained for. He shifted in his seat. He couldn't see the attraction of it.

After the sermon, however, his attention was captured by something in the service for the very first time. People were passing plates of bread down the pews. He grabbed the bulletin, which said it was called communion. After Corinne received her bread from Becky, she selected another piece, turned to Marcus, and placed it in his hand.

Folding his fingers over it she said, "Marcus, this bread represents the body of Christ, which was broken for you for the forgiveness of sins. Take, eat, and remember."

Marcus felt his whole body tremble slightly at the solemnity of her words. He opened his hand and looked at the piece of bread, and then he looked at Corinne. She raised her eyebrows in encouragement, and he picked it up and put it in his mouth. Then she handed him the plate and he passed it along to the server.

Next Corinne received a small cup of juice from Becky, then turned and gave another of the same to him. "This represents the blood of Christ, which was shed for you for the forgiveness of sins. Take, drink, and remember."

Marcus heard nothing more for the remainder of the service.

Becky and Corinne chatted together as they moved toward the exit. Daniel was talking with some friends up ahead. Marcus simply followed along, lost in his own thoughts. As they waited in a bottleneck at the door, Roger approached and touched him on the shoulder. "I was wondering if you'd have breakfast with me tomorrow morning?" he asked. "We could hit the diner early before we each head to work. What do you say?"

Marcus was startled. "Yeah, sure. But why?"

Roger's eyes were kind. "Let's just say I've been where you are." Marcus stared at him, unable to say a word. "Maddie's at seven?" Roger prompted.

Marcus nodded and then somehow managed to stumble out the door. The breeze hit his face and jolted him awake. His heart started pounding and his hands began to tremble. He made his excuses to Daniel and the two women, and then bolted for his car, leaving his friends surprised and perplexed in the parking lot.

As soon as he pulled into his driveway, Marcus let down and collapsed over the steering wheel. *What the hell just happened?* Was he losing his mind? Marcus wasn't used to being taken by surprise. He always had a snappy comeback in every conversation, and yet here he was rendered speechless, repeatedly, inside that building. It was making him crazy. He shouldn't go back.

He dropped his keys on the table inside the door, skipped lunch, and tore into mowing his lawn instead. It didn't take long. After it was finished, he was still off-kilter, so he got out the string trimmer, and then the hedge clippers, and even the weed spray. By mid-afternoon his yard was manicured almost to death.

Afterward, he collapsed onto the outdoor sofa on his back deck. The physical exertion had helped calm him down, but it hadn't removed the sneaking suspicion that had been plaguing him all afternoon: even if he never did go back, it wouldn't matter. He couldn't undo what had already been done.

Whatever that was.

The sun was hot, and he was in desperate need of a shower, but he didn't move right away. The breeze was pleasant, and it cooled his sweaty skin. He grew drowsy and the gentle stupor settled his mind. When hunger drove him indoors late that afternoon, enough time had passed for him to feel that he was reasonably in control of himself once again.

It was only a short while later, though, as he was fixing himself a plate of food, that an unbidden thought crept into his mind. He had missed lunch with Corinne, but he was looking forward to breakfast with Roger.

Seven a.m. came pretty early for Marcus to arrive anywhere, but whatever it was that made him look forward to the meeting also compelled him to get to Maddie's on time. He pulled open the door and saw Roger chatting with people in one of the booths by the front windows. As soon as Roger saw him, he excused himself and came straight over.

"Good morning, Marcus! Great to see you." He shook Marcus's hand, and they sat down at a table in the middle of the diner.

"You too, Roger." Suddenly Marcus grew self-conscious. He didn't know what to expect out of this meeting, and that made him uncomfortable. He grabbed the menu and perused it, never mind that he knew it by heart. Roger followed suit, and after a brief moment, Maddie appeared, coffee pot in hand.

"Well now, isn't this a surprise!" she drawled as she filled two coffee cups.

"Good morning, Miss Maddie!" Roger greeted her as a friend. "You're looking very well. That knee behaving itself?"

"So far so good, but it's still early." Maddie clucked her tongue at the conclusion of this announcement and turned to Marcus.

"Good morning, Maddie," he said, his voice timid.

Maddie eyed him warily. "Never seen you here this early before."

"That would be my doing," Roger said. "After church yesterday, I invited him to join me this morning."

She raised an eyebrow. "You going to church now?" Marcus nodded mutely. She looked him over and then concluded, "Will wonders never cease!" This made Marcus laugh out loud, and the tension within him broke. Maddie turned back toward Roger. "You fellas know what you want?"

The two men placed their orders and as Maddie moved to the next table, Roger picked up his coffee cup and blew on it. "I'm sure I left you quite curious after church yesterday."

"You could say that."

Roger took a sip of the hot brew. "I could be way off base, but I had the strong impression that the communion service packed quite a punch for you."

Marcus didn't respond but just watched the other man, wondering how on earth he could have known that.

Roger set down his coffee cup. "Your first one?"

"Yeah." And then he blurted out, "All of it is new to me. I'd never been to church in my life before three weeks ago." He looked away, unsure what the older man would think, and unwilling to see it in his face.

"That's where I've been," Roger said.

Marcus flinched. Had he heard correctly?

Roger continued. "That's right. I used to know nothing about any of it either." He then fell silent and took another sip of coffee as Marcus contemplated his words.

How could that be? Roger was always talking about God! Marcus's thoughts were in a jumble and once again, he couldn't figure out what to say. Just as he was about to try, Maddie brought two steaming plates of bacon, scrambled eggs, toast, and hash browns and set them in front of the men. "Enjoy your breakfast," she said and returned to the kitchen.

Marcus grabbed his napkin and unrolled the silverware. He was about to dig in when he heard Roger say, "Would it be all right with you if I prayed for our meal before we begin?"

"Oh. Sure, of course." He dropped the silverware, and glancing around, put his hands in his lap. He looked at Roger, who bowed his head. Marcus jerked his head downward, but he didn't close his eyes.

Roger kept his prayer brief. "Father, we thank you for this food and for new friendships. I am grateful that You make yourself known to us in Your good time. Amen."

"Amen." Relieved, Marcus picked up his fork and took a bite of eggs. Roger tucked his napkin into his lap and did likewise. "You a native?" he asked, and then gestured around himself when Marcus looked up at him.

"Of Ohio, yes. But not of Sutton."

"Same. Most of my family lives in Ohio too, although they're spread all over."

"My brother doesn't live far, but he drives truck, so he's gone a lot."

"You close with him?"

Marcus was spreading strawberry jam on his toast but paused at this question. "Yeah. We took care of each other growing up. We had to."

Roger closed his eyes. "It's a good thing you had each other. I was on my own, and I didn't do such a great job taking care of myself." He took a bite of bacon and was silent as he chewed. "I was well on my way to an early grave, the way I was living."

Marcus leaned back in his chair. "I never would've guessed that."

"It's true."

"What happened to change it?"

Roger gathered a bite of hash browns on his fork. "The only thing I can say is that for some reason, God intervened." He looked up, piercing Marcus with his eyes. "Every day of my life, I'm grateful to Him for that."

The men ate in silence for a few moments, each lost in thought. Marcus was trying to pull it all together but having no luck. "I don't get it. You said He intervened. What did He do?"

"He sent His people into my life when I was at my very worst and they showed me His love." Roger's eyes misted over as he remembered. "I was busy living my life, doing my own thing. Thought church people were nice enough but a little quirky, you know?"

Marcus might have been known to think similar thoughts from time to time, even about his own good friends, Daniel and Becky. Even about the man sitting across from him.

"Then I met someone and went to church for the first time ever. I hadn't a clue what was going on there. Didn't think much about it, to be honest. All I knew was that I wanted to be where she was."

Marcus dropped his head. "Ah."

Roger smiled. "Another similar place I've been."

Marcus took a breath, hesitated, and then plunged forward. "Daniel and Becky have been inviting me to church for years, and I've always turned them down. 'Til now."

"Well, there are worse reasons to start going to church than for a woman." Roger chuckled at Marcus's surprise. "When God wants to make Himself known to us, He uses all kinds of means to do so. Even a woman."

Is that what this is? God trying to get my attention? Marcus thought he'd been trying to get Corinne's attention. He wasn't sure how he felt about this. He pushed the uncomfortable thought aside and instead said, "Making Himself known; that's what you said in your prayer, too."

"That's right." Roger watched him and then leaned forward and rested his elbows on the table. "I had the sense that's what He was doing with you yesterday morning. Making Himself known."

Marcus shifted in his seat and then waved his fork in the air. "I don't know why He'd want to. I've got nothing to offer."

"Neither did I. But God doesn't seek us because He needs something from us. He seeks us because He wants a relationship with us."

As Marcus was pondering this inconceivable statement, Maddie appeared and cleared their plates. She offered more coffee, but both men declined.

"It's a lot to take in," Roger said.

Marcus raised an eyebrow. "Yeah."

Roger pulled out his wallet and put some bills on the table. Marcus reached for his as well, but Roger stopped him. "My treat," he said.

"You don't have to do that," Marcus protested.

"No, it's my pleasure. You can get the next one." He winked and then pushed back his chair. "How about next Monday?"

Marcus's mouth dropped open in surprise. Then he heard himself say, "I'll be here."

9

Corinne, meanwhile, was paying the price for her impromptu trip out of town. It's not that she didn't sightsee on the weekends, because she did. It's just that she didn't usually do it on the first Saturday of the month. Usually, she worked that Saturday.

Everybody wanted their financial statements as soon as possible, and that meant a flurry of reports and reviews and reconciliations all packed into a few short days. Now that she thought about it, it was probably time to hire again. The load had become pretty heavy. Corinne made a note to prioritize a search, but not until after month end.

For now, she just had to get through it. Since she'd chosen to play over the weekend, she had to put in the time all Sunday after worship and several evenings that week. She dug in and worked hard and by the end of the day Thursday, was caught up and ready to do something fun again. That's when she remembered where she was living and that she needed to plan ahead. *Drat it.* It wasn't a habit yet.

A quick internet search netted nothing within reasonable driving distance. In the city she could have had her evening sorted out in the time it took to warm a plate of food.

Corinne laid her phone on the counter and pulled open the refrigerator door. She needed a list for times like this: go-to activities in a small town. Or at least in the area. Was there an open gym somewhere nearby? A random game of frisbee golf down at the park? Maybe she could join the neighborhood kids in their games. Wouldn't that be a hoot? She wondered if they'd even let her.

Then she realized she'd been staring into her refrigerator for several minutes. Annoyed, she shut the door and grabbed her purse. There was no way she was going to let her new circumstances get the best of her. Nope, she was going to figure this out. And she'd start this evening by taking a drive. See what she could see. Get to know her surroundings a little better.

She stopped in front of the mirror to take stock. Her casual t-shirt, shorts, and sandals were a perk of working from home, especially when she had no meetings. She dismissed her reflection as acceptable for wandering about the countryside and headed out the door.

First things first, though. Supper. A sandwich would do. As she stood at the counter waiting for her sub to toast, another curious thing happened. Her phone pinged with a text from Becky.

What're you up to this evening?

Not much. You?

Same. You should come over. Dan's going out and I need girl talk!

Be right there!

Cool! Corinne was delighted. She hadn't thought about calling Becky! Hanging out with friends wasn't on her usual list of activities. A fact which made it even more curious that she was so thrilled with the invitation.

With her evening plans now established, she paid for the sandwich and carried it with her. It took all of three minutes to drive to Daniel and Becky's house. *Definitely on the small-town perks list, that.*

Her friends lived in a quaint, two-story century home with a wrap-around porch. It was huge, as she learned on her grand tour. There were four bedrooms on the second floor with a walkout deck from the master. The third floor was an unfinished attic. "A work in progress," Becky called it. Back on the main floor, she guided Corinne through the twists and turns of the myriad rooms. "This one is nice for gatherings. Sometimes we host Bible study or even the youth group."

"This is amazing, Becky. You guys have so much room here!"

A shadow crossed Becky's face but was quickly replaced by her warm smile. "We do," she agreed, "and we try to use it for good purpose as much as we can. Now come on! Let's go sit on the deck and you can eat your sandwich."

10

Off-balance. That's how Marcus had been feeling all week. Not a single thing in his life was going as he expected it to right now. Everything caught him off guard.

If only he hadn't gone that one more Sunday, things would be just fine. As it was, nothing was fine. Nothing was like it was supposed to be, not even at work.

Take his Thursday afternoon appointment, for example. Abigail Fredrickson. She was done being married and ready to make her soon-to-be ex-husband pay through the nose for his many indiscretions. She was angry when she walked in, and Marcus's distractedness served only to stoke the furnace. "Mr. Hunter, are you even listening? I thought you were the toughest divorce lawyer around, but you haven't heard a word I've said!"

"I'm sorry, Mrs. Fredrickson—"

"DON'T call me that!" she thundered.

"Abigail. Of course." He grabbed his pen and forced himself to concentrate, outlining the broad strokes of her complaint. Along with everything else, she was positive her husband was hiding money from her and wanted to make sure it was found before time came for the divorce settlement. Marcus asked all the right questions and made all the right plans, and Mrs. Fredrickson—er, Abigail—left his office confident that Mr. Fredrickson would be stripped of his very manhood by the time they finished with him.

Typically, Marcus was confident of the same outcome and had no qualms about sticking it to the man or woman sitting across the aisle. But today Marcus was off-balance. And for the life of him he couldn't remember why it was he ever took pleasure in helping to rip people's lives apart.

The rest of the afternoon was a wash, so Marcus gave it up and went home. That wasn't any better though, and he found himself rattling around his empty house like a ghost, unable to recall what it was that he normally did with his time.

About suppertime he grabbed his phone and texted Daniel.

Dude, wanna shoot hoops?

Kiddin'? Meet ya there.

Most people went to the nice courts at the rec center to play, so that's why Marcus and Daniel always went to the junior high—it was deserted. Daniel was already laying a few in when Marcus pulled up. He grabbed the ball from the back seat and headed to the court. "What's up," he called.

Daniel lifted his chin in greeting, and for a few minutes they shot easy and dribbled round, shaking out their muscles and warming up. Pretty soon they ditched one of the balls and launched into an intense game of *21*. They spoke little, and before long both were sweaty and out of breath.

Marcus attacked the game with a vengeance and soon was up 18 to 10. He rebounded the ball and took it out to the three-point line. He crouched low and dribbled, eyeing Daniel. Then he feinted right and went left for a layup. Score.

That put him at twenty.

"Oh man." Daniel breathed hard as he retrieved the ball and smacked it. "You are kickin' my ass tonight."

Marcus just smirked from the free throw line, hands on his hips. "Yeah, well Becky can comfort you later. What's she doing tonight anyway?"

"Oh, she and Corinne are hanging out on the back deck. Girl talk." He drilled the ball at his friend.

"Oof." Marcus grunted when it hit him in the gut and fell away to the ground. He looked up at Daniel in surprise.

Daniel smiled real slow.

"Corinne's at your house?"

"Take your shot, dude."

"Right now?"

"Sooner the better. Let's get this game over with." Daniel snickered as Marcus stomped off to retrieve the ball from the edge of the court. When he returned to the free throw line, he bounced the ball a few times, his thoughts elsewhere.

"Shoot the damn ball, Marcus! Or can't you close the deal?" Daniel taunted.

"You wish!" he snapped. Marcus gripped the ball hard. One last quick bounce, a little spin, and then he relaxed, letting his forearms come to rest against his hips. He exhaled, brought the ball up above his head, and let it fly.

Both guys watched as it flew in a perfect arc toward the basket, with just the right amount of backspin—and then bounced off the rim. "Crap," Marcus muttered. Daniel scrambled for the ball and proceeded to trounce his friend within the next five minutes.

They collapsed on the bench, panting heavily. Marcus rubbed his arm across his forehead. Then he shoved Daniel on the shoulder and said, "Dirty play, man."

"Hey, you asked." Daniel sniggered and pulled a couple bottles of water from his bag. He handed one to Marcus, who twisted the lid and took a long pull. He sniffed and looked at the bottle.

"I sure could use a beer right about now."

Daniel tipped his head. "I've got a couple of cold ones in the fridge." He glanced at Marcus. "At home."

Marcus looked sideways at his friend. "Yeah?"

Daniel grabbed his bag and got up from the bench. "Let's go."

Daniel dumped his bag in the foyer and led the way to the kitchen. He grabbed two beers from the fridge and handed one to Marcus. They popped the tops, and each took a swig.

"Aw, yeah," Marcus said. "That hits the spot. You know, I haven't had a beer in a month."

Daniel raised an eyebrow. "Why not?"

"I dunno. Haven't thought about it."

"Huh." Daniel eyed his friend. "That's not a bad thing."

"Probably not." He lifted his chin toward the sliding glass door. "Lead the way."

Daniel grinned. "Make plenty of noise so they know we're coming."

As they crashed and thundered through the house, and then slid open the door to the deck, Becky turned to Corinne and said, "I do believe my husband is home."

"Knock, knock," Daniel called. "You girls want some company?"

Marcus stopped halfway through the door, breathless once again when he saw Corinne. She was wearing a t-shirt and—Lord have mercy—shorts. She had kicked off her sandals and was leaning sideways against the arm of her chair, chin resting in her hand, one foot tucked underneath her, brushing the toes of the other against the wooden slats of the deck.

When Marcus stopped in the doorway, she straightened up and lowered both feet to the ground.

Daniel leaned over Becky and gave her a big wet kiss. "Hey, baby."

"Oh lordy, Daniel, you smell! Get away!" She pushed at him with her fingertip. "Ugh!"

Corinne's eyes sparkled as she observed their antics, and Marcus was mesmerized yet again.

"You wanna come out and shut the door, big guy?" Daniel drawled.

"Hmm?" Marcus tore his gaze away from Corinne to look at Daniel. Daniel just raised an eyebrow at him. "Oh, right. The door. Sorry." He slid it closed and took a seat in another of the deck chairs.

In a few moments, when he'd regained his composure, he looked pointedly at Corinne and patted the armrest of his chair. "Ahh."

She just rolled her eyes and looked away, but he saw the hint of a smile playing about her lips. Marcus soaked it in and then looked down at his drink. *Better than beer, that.* He set the bottle on the table.

"So, who won?" Becky wanted to know.

"I did," Daniel crowed. "Whupped his ass."

"Daniel," Becky chided.

"He cheated," Marcus intoned.

Daniel snorted. "I won fair and square, brother." Marcus sniffed and turned away, examining his fingernails.

"What'd you play?" Corinne looked back and forth between the guys.

"*21*," Marcus said. "Basketball."

"I know what *21* is!"

Marcus raised his hands and his eyebrows in mock concession, but the smirk which accompanied it told a different story. This time Corinne glared at him before looking away, but he could tell she wasn't really annoyed. Rather, she was doing everything in her power to focus her attention elsewhere. That was fine with him; it gave him license to stare. She fidgeted in her seat, crossing and recrossing her ankles, scrunching her toes as she did so. It was pure agony to behold.

"Summer is just the best." That was Becky, breaking the companionable silence that had descended upon them. Marcus silently agreed. Shorts were a beautiful thing.

Corinne turned toward Becky. "What's your favorite part?"

Becky stretched and rested her hands along the top edge of her chair. "Everything! Lazy days, gorgeous evenings, slower pace."

Marcus shifted in his seat. "Says the woman who has summers off. The rest of us have to work, you know. Even in summer."

"Hey! I put my time in during the school year, and plenty of it. Besides, none of you has to deal with a room full of rambunctious kids all day long."

"Aww, you love it and you know it, Bec." Daniel smiled at his wife.

She pursed her lips at her husband, her eyes full. "I do at that."

Marcus had kept his eyes fixed on Corinne during this exchange, so he saw the shift in her countenance—from purposeful avoidance of him to contemplation of Becky. *What the devil is she thinking?* Marcus had to know. He patted his pocket but found it empty. "Hey, Corinne." She looked up at him. "Penny," he said, and tapped his head.

She pressed her lips together and shook her head.

"Why not?" he asked.

She answered with raised eyebrows, her eyes serious and penetrating. *Even more curious.* But this thought was soon eclipsed by another: twice this evening she had known, instantaneously, what he meant, and just as quickly her own response.

Twice. He leaned his head back against the chair, surprised to discover how satisfying it was to be understood, with or without words.

Daniel and Becky were chatting together about the cookout they were hosting on Saturday, when Becky turned to Corinne and said, "You are coming, aren't you, Corinne?"

Corinne turned toward her, confused. "Sorry. Coming to what?"

"Our cookout on Saturday. Celebrating the end of the school year."

"Oh! Sounds fun. I didn't know about it."

"I didn't tell you? I'm sorry! You have to come. It's a couple of my teacher friends from church and their families." Becky stopped and looked at her. "You don't already have plans, do you?"

Corinne's eyes crinkled as she smiled at her friend. "Nothing set it stone."

"Oh, good," Becky said. "So, you'll be here?"

"Absolutely. What can I bring?"

As the two women discussed food and plans and guests, Daniel turned to Marcus and said, "You know you're always invited."

"Yeah, I know."

"So maybe you'll take me up on this invitation now, too?" Daniel asked.

Marcus chuckled. "I might."

"Good man."

11

Topping Corinne's new list, which she entitled, *Things to Do While Living in the Middle of Nowhere,* was

    1. spend time with friends

Thursday had been fantastic. One friend, a group of friends, it didn't seem to matter. She liked it. Not to mention the fact that it was new and different, at least for her.

What hadn't been fantastic, or at least not comfortable, was Marcus's obvious appreciation of her legs. Not to say that she minded being appreciated. It was just that, well, she hadn't expected the guys to be around. She would have dressed differently had she known. Corinne didn't ever make a habit of drawing attention to herself, but it was more than that. An appreciation of her legs simply didn't add much to his recommendation. Physical attraction might be gratifying, but it was also easy. And it often muddied the waters.

Whatever. It didn't matter right now. Corinne had more important things to sort out. Such as how to fill part of a Saturday before an evening social engagement, which was another new and different thing in her life.

It's not that she was a wallflower, or antisocial; she just didn't crave company. Hadn't, anyway. She never needed much of it, even growing up, and if she were honest, college was a bit of an overload. Now however, after six years of being on her own, independent, free, answering to no one but herself, she found she was ready for a little society once again.

Determined not to make the same mistake twice when it came to planning out her travels, she didn't wait. She mapped out her Saturday sightseeing plans as soon as she got home from Becky's Thursday evening.

Early Saturday morning she headed to Seneca Caverns near Bellevue. Navigation routed her through farm country, where she saw nothing but fields and an occasional house surrounded by barns and gardens, cows and horses.

That tour was only about an hour long, so afterward she drove into Bellevue proper, passing by Flat Rock on her way. The tiny community and care center was tucked along a highway out in the middle of nowhere. She wondered what could have possessed them to locate the facility in such a remote place instead of in a city, near resources and opportunities.

Once in Bellevue, she perused the train museum. Her favorite part was wandering through the train cars themselves. She'd never been on a train; in her travels, she always preferred the autonomy of her own personal vehicle.

At noon she stopped in a nearby park—also empty—to enjoy the lunch she had packed. While there, she checked her phone to see what else was in the area, since what she'd done so far hadn't taken much time. Lyme Village wasn't far, so she drove up there.

She joined a tour but determined it'd be good to come back for one of their events, where they had activities. She pinned it on her phone and then typed in "home". The navigation software took her there by a different route than the one she'd taken that morning. Every few miles there was a little town, and there were homes scattered all along the way in between.

It was much different from the morning drive; she never quite felt like she was out in the boonies as she had earlier. Once she got home, she did a bit of research on the state and learned just how densely populated it was. *What an odd mix*, she thought. *Huge tracts of farmland, Amish and Mennonite populations, and yet so much developed and populated space too.* Numerous big cities and tons of colleges, but all you had to do was blink and you could find yourself slowing down for a horse and buggy!

It had been a good day, and she still had the cookout to look forward to. She showered, and then in pondering her closet decided on a summer dress and sandals. That would be more comfortable than shorts, for lots of reasons.

Grabbing the potato salad she'd made the night before, she headed out the door and over to Daniel and Becky's. She pulled into the driveway, the first to arrive.

"Am I too early?" she questioned as Becky opened the door.

"Not at all!" Becky said. "You can help me in the kitchen." She grabbed Corinne's hand and pulled her that direction, chattering as she went.

Daniel entered from the back deck and greeted Corinne. "So glad you could join us instead of heading out to explore the world!"

"Ha! Already been and done." Daniel's eyes lit up in surprise. Then the doorbell rang, and he left to answer it.

Before long all the guests had arrived: two other young couples from church, each with children in tow—and Marcus. After pondering the guest list, Corinne dismissed her thoughts on the subject and set about learning the names of all the children. It was a long-distance undertaking, as they were already engaged in a backyard football game with the men.

After depositing all the food items in the fridge, Becky led the group of women through the sliding door onto the deck and called to her husband, "Why don't you guys go across to the school? There's more room for your game."

"You ladies need to come cheer us on!" Marcus called. "Otherwise, we don't stand a chance against these fierce competitors." He growled and extended his hands like claws, pretending to attack his prey. The children squealed and dashed across the yard with Marcus in hot pursuit. The women grabbed lawn chairs and followed the boisterous crew to the large grassy field next to Sutton Elementary. Corinne might have opted to join in the fun, except that she hadn't dressed for it. *Shorts might have been better, after all,* she thought. Then again, she figured it was best to follow the lead of the other women and spend time getting to know them.

"Is this where you teach, Becky?" she asked as the women settled their chairs in a shaded grassy area.

"It is."

"Well, that's handy!"

"Sometimes. But when it snows or rains I either have to tromp through the mess or walk all the way around the block to avoid it, so I end up driving most of the time anyway."

"Plus, what teacher doesn't have a ton of stuff to carry back and forth every day?" Elizabeth said. "I teach at the high school. Language arts." Elizabeth and her husband Thomas had two of the children who were playing in the field.

"That's true," Becky agreed. "Carrying books and papers makes walking a whole lot less pleasant."

"Pfft, having kids makes going anywhere less pleasant!" Sabrina complained. "It takes me at least a half an hour just to get out the door to go grocery shopping." Sabrina was a full-time mom, her husband the teacher in the family.

"Amen to that," Elizabeth agreed. "Everything's more expensive with kids, too—meals, travel, clothing. Don't get me wrong; I love my kids." She wrinkled her nose at Becky and Corinne. "Just enjoy your freedom while you've got it."

Becky said nothing. Corinne had no idea what to say either and instead turned her attention to the game. She could understand their perspective. They were in the thick of family life and would relish even the briefest moment of what they had called freedom. She had to admit, she loved her freedom.

And yet, she was surprised to realize, there was a tiny sliver of something else in the mix. *Was that a pang of longing?*

After the football game, everyone trooped back to Daniel and Becky's. The guys gathered around the grill as Daniel fired it up and cooked the burgers. The women brought the rest of the food out from the kitchen, and soon everyone was enjoying a meal together in the backyard. The children lounged on the steps and the adults arranged themselves on the deck.

"May I?" Marcus gestured toward the seat next to Corinne.

"Of course." She set down her hamburger and nibbled on chips instead. Marcus was trying to arrange his drink without upsetting his plate. When he finished the task, he picked up his burger and took a huge bite, then looked up at her and grinned.

Amused, she said, "Looked like you were enjoying yourself out there." She looked toward the school.

Marcus swallowed. "Probably more than I should have been."

"Not at all." Corinne objected. "The kids loved it."

"Yeah, I guess they did," he agreed.

Corinne gave her burger another try and scrutinized him as she chewed. "You like kids," she concluded.

A flash of surprise crossed his face, and then he set down his sandwich and fiddled with his own chips. "Don't have a ton of experience with them, but yeah, I guess I've always enjoyed my nephews, throwing the football, whatever."

"That's cool. What—"

They were startled from their conversation by a loud burst of laughter from the group. It was the women. Elizabeth and Sabrina, to be exact, but not Becky. She was listening to her friends, but she didn't join in their chatter.

Corinne now divided her attention between observing Becky and chatting with Marcus. By the time their plates were empty, she was convinced that something was bothering her friend.

When the two families with kids called it an evening so they could get the little ones to bed for church in the morning, Corinne stuck around to help Becky clean up. They carried platters and utensils to the kitchen. Daniel and Marcus stayed in the backyard putting away chairs and toys and cleaning up the deck. Corinne started dishwater in the sink.

"You don't have to do that," Becky protested.

"I don't mind; we didn't get to talk much this evening."

Becky said nothing and turned away to wipe the counters. When she came back to the sink, Corinne tried again. "Is everything okay? You were very quiet this evening." Becky rubbed the cloth back and forth over the same clean spot. When she looked up at Corinne, there were tears in her eyes.

"It's so hard." Her voice was choked. "I love Elizabeth and Sabrina, but sometimes it's hard to be around them and their families." She stopped and drew in a shaky breath. "Daniel and I have never been able to have children," she whispered.

"Oh, Becky." Corinne was stunned—and then rocked by a wave of guilt. She had never even considered their family life—or lack of it. She dried her hands and pulled Becky into a hug. She could feel as well as hear her friend sobbing. "I'm so sorry," she murmured.

The only sound for the next few moments was Becky's sniffles. When she pulled away, she got a tissue to blow her nose. Then she gestured around the house. "We bought this place and started fixing it up, intending to fill it with children. Nine years later, here it still sits, huge and empty." Her eyes pleaded with Corinne, as if sharing this heartache with her could somehow make it go away.

They sat down at the table and Corinne reached out to squeeze Becky's hands. At a complete loss for how to offer any comfort, she was startled to hear these words come out of her mouth. "Let's pray together, okay?"

Becky bowed her head. Occasional sobs continued to break through as she struggled to control her emotions. Corinne took a deep breath, closed her eyes, and then began. "Oh, Father..."

12

Daniel and Marcus disposed of the last bits of trash from the party and headed toward the door. Just as Marcus was about to slide the glass open to go inside, Daniel stopped him. "Hold on."

"What's up?" Marcus asked, and then he looked inside. There, sitting at the table, were Corinne and Becky, hands held, heads bowed, eyes closed.

He looked at Daniel in surprise, whose eyes were serious. "Let's give them a minute," Daniel said.

They turned back to sit on the steps of the deck. "Are they praying?" Marcus asked.

"Looks that way."

"What about?" Immediately he felt embarrassed. "Sorry. That was a dumb question."

"No, it's okay. Only natural to be curious." But he said no more.

Marcus was curious, uncomfortably so. He and Corinne had had a nice, albeit brief, conversation that evening, just the two of them. But this stuff was out of his realm.

Daniel was studying the sky. "I'm glad you came tonight," he said.

"Yeah, me too."

"Not as lame as you thought it would be?"

"No," he admitted. "I had a good time."

"I'm glad to hear it." Movement from inside the house caught their attention. "Looks like we can head in," Daniel said, so the two of them got up.

Corinne was gathering her belongings as they came through. Becky's eyes were red, and she was still sniffling. Marcus wasn't sure what he should or shouldn't say, but he knew he wanted to say thank you, so he did.

"Becky, thanks so much for inviting me. I appreciate it, and I had a great time."

"Of course, Marcus!" Becky came and gave him a big hug. "You know you're always welcome." She smiled up at him, and his heart was touched. Becky was always loving and kind, even in the midst of her own sorrow, whatever it was.

"Thank you for that."

Corinne offered her thanks to Daniel but with a handshake instead of a hug. Then the four of them moved toward the door. It was, therefore, inevitable that Marcus and Corinne left the house at the same time. Corinne was quiet, and Marcus was hesitant to break her silence given what he had just witnessed.

When they reached her car, however, he said, "Here, let me get the door for you."

"Oh, thank you." She deposited her salad and her purse on the seat. Marcus closed the door and Corinne moved to the driver's side. "We'll see you in the morning."

"Er," Marcus stumbled momentarily, but then recovered. "Right! Yes, see you at church." Corinne waved and then got in her car, started the motor, and drove away.

Marcus stood rooted to the spot for a full minute, realizing he'd just committed to another Sunday in church. Part of him was annoyed at how easily that had happened. How come he couldn't get it together enough to snag a phone number and a date from this woman? Another greater part of him, however, was remembering some words his new acquaintance Roger had spoken less than a week ago:

I wanted to be where she was.

Marcus's shoulders slumped, and he shook his head. He knew he was beat, because the fact of the matter was, he felt the same way.

Having admitted defeat on the issue of church attendance, Marcus was up early the next morning, whistling as he got ready to go. He wasn't the type to spend time lamenting the past.

He slapped on aftershave and contemplated what it would be like to have Corinne do that for him. He donned a dress shirt and pants and wondered what she'd be wearing today and what she'd look like without—.

Quickly he pushed those thoughts aside, realizing almost too late that they would only get him into trouble this morning. Instead, he thought about the cookout.

It had been surprisingly pleasant. He'd always declined those invitations, figuring a social gathering of church people couldn't have anything to recommend it. He was wrong; it had been fun. They were lighthearted, not at all dour, and the conversation was, well, normal.

Scratch that. It wasn't normal. Or, he should say, it wasn't typical. *What was it then?* Clean, he guessed. Family-oriented. That was refreshing, he realized with no small amount of surprise. And he had to admit Corinne was right: he did love playing with those kids. It made him realize how much he missed that from when his nephews were younger. *I should go see them. It's been a while.*

Marcus ran his fingers through his hair and brushed the unruly waves across his forehead. He stared into the mirror, thinking about Becky and Corinne praying. That had been a whole different thing from the rest of the evening. Even Daniel had been solemn when they discovered the two women with their heads bowed. *Why was that? Was he annoyed?* Marcus didn't think so. *What could it have been, then?* The realization struck him that whatever was going on, he was the only one of the four not privy to it.

Not quite certain how he felt about that, he turned away from the mirror, donned his suit coat, and left the house.

As he got out of his car in the parking lot at the church a few minutes later, he saw Corinne pulling in, so he waited to walk in with her. "Good morning," he called as she exited her vehicle.

"Morning! You enjoy the cookout last night?" Corinne asked.

"Yeah, I did."

"You sound surprised."

"A little, I guess. I'd never been to one of Dan and Bec's cookouts before."

"I figured you were a permanent fixture."

"They always invite. I've just never taken them up on it before."

"Hmm. Why not?"

"Er—"

Thankfully, Daniel and Becky arrived at just that moment, and Becky rushed across the parking lot to Corinne, her husband following at a more leisurely pace. "Morning!" Becky said. She slipped her arm through Corinne's. "How are you doing?"

"I'm good! But how about you?"

"I'm better." She wrinkled her nose and then whispered, "Thank you."

"Anytime," Corinne whispered back.

Marcus held open the door for the four of them to enter the building. Daniel offered a small, "Morning," as he passed by, but nothing else. Marcus was intrigued yet again by the exchange between Becky and Corinne. *What the devil was going on?*

Even though he managed to finagle a seat next to Corinne again, he didn't pay much attention to that fact. Instead, he continued to obsess over the girls' secret. It wasn't until the sermon that he was startled from his reverie.

"Hear the words of Matthew chapter 18, verses 12-14," said the pastor. "'What do you think? If any man has a hundred sheep, and one of them goes astray, will he not leave the ninety-nine on the mountains, and go and search for the one that is lost? And if it turns out that he finds it, truly I say to you, he rejoices over it more than over the ninety-nine that have not gone astray. So it is not the will of your Father who is in heaven for one of these little ones to perish.'"

The pastor looked up from the text. "From this we see that sometimes a sheep of the fold wanders away. Likewise, sometimes we wander away, and our Savior wants to bring us back into His care. Others of us have never yet experienced what it feels like to be cared for by the Good Shepherd, to be part of the fold. If that is you, Jesus desires to care for you, too, to bring you peace, comfort, security, and love."

Marcus frowned. He'd love to have those things in his life. In fact, he realized, it's what he'd always been searching for. But this made no sense to him. What did sheep and shepherds have to do with it?

Marcus was oblivious to the entire rest of the service and the slow shuffle out the door. In fact, he was so caught up in his musings that he paid little attention as each of his friends took their leave. When he came to, Daniel and Becky were waving goodbye as they drove away, and he was standing alone among the remaining parked cars. He picked his way through them until he reached his own.

The sermon was still fresh in his mind the next morning when he arrived at Maddie's Diner. Even though it was a few minutes before seven, Roger still had him beat. Marcus wondered how early he'd have to arrive to best the older man, and as Roger greeted him, it was as if he'd read his thoughts.

"Some friends I only get to see at 6:30 in the morning here at the diner, so I do." Roger's smile always lit up his entire face. It was warm and genuine. He gestured to a table, a different one than last week, and the two men sat down. Maddie appeared with coffee and gave Marcus a brief look as she poured. "Morning."

"Good morning, Maddie. How're you doing?" Marcus asked.

"Right as rain, and yourself?"

"Not too bad. Thanks for asking." Marcus smiled at her and she looked at him suspiciously. She turned to Roger and filled his coffee cup.

"You know what you're having this morning?"

"As a matter of fact, I do. Marcus?"

Marcus agreed, and the two men placed their orders without bothering to look at the menu. As Maddie headed back to the kitchen, Roger asked, "So, how was your week, Marcus?"

Marcus took a deep breath. "It was, uh...different."

"Different how?"

Marcus rubbed his fingers over his jaw as he thought. "I'm used to having the answers, you know? And if I don't, then finding them. It's what lawyers do. But church, and I'll be honest, even our conversation last week..." He shook his head. "Well, let's just say they rattled me. In fact, I almost blew a new client meeting Thursday afternoon."

Roger grimaced. "Ooh, that's not good."

"No, it's not. But I managed to pull it together." Both men fell silent as they tested their coffee. The early morning chatter in the diner was different than noontime, Marcus noticed. It was more relaxed. He looked around the room and saw a lot of older men who no longer had to punch a clock. They had all the time in the world. Lunch was the business crowd who had deadlines to meet.

"Did you hear the message yesterday morning?" Roger wanted to know.

"Some of it," Marcus hedged.

"What did you hear?"

"The preacher was talking about sheep." Marcus lifted his palm in the air.

"Indeed. What do you think it meant?"

Marcus had no idea. It seemed like craziness to him.

Maddie delivered two steaming plates of food to the table. Pancakes with sausage links for Marcus, and biscuits and gravy for Roger. They each unfolded their silverware and placed the napkins in their laps, but this time, Marcus didn't dive right into his food.

"Shall we pray?" Roger asked.

Marcus bowed his head.

"Heavenly Father," Roger said. "We ask that you bless this food and the hands that prepared it. Thank you for always providing exactly what we need. In Jesus' name. Amen."

Roger picked up his fork and looked at Marcus. "Any ideas?"

Marcus doused his pancakes with syrup. "Nope."

"It's challenging when the Bible talks in terms we don't typically use. People back then would have understood perfectly, because sheep were their livelihood."

Marcus tipped his head to the side as he thought this over. Roger continued. "If we were to think of it in terms of our own life and times, perhaps we could say we were talking about clients. They're our livelihood, right, and if they start wandering away, we're going to want to bring them back."

"I suppose. But one's not a big deal if you have ninety-nine others."

Roger pursed his lips. "What did you do on Thursday when you almost blew it with that new client?"

"I got my shit together and did my job." Marcus flinched. "Sorry." He was embarrassed that he'd spoken thus in front of Roger.

But the older man waved it away. "Why did you do that?"

"I didn't want to lose the client."

"Why not?"

"Bad press," he admitted.

"So that one client was important?"

"Yeah."

"Likewise, the one sheep was important to the shepherd."

Marcus swirled his fork in the syrup on top of his pancakes. "It's not the same scenario."

"No, it isn't. Not exactly. But they both illustrate the importance of *the one* to the one in charge."

"Okay," Marcus drew out the word as he thought.

Roger spoke again. "Bear with me; let's keep going with the sheep analogy. If the ninety-nine sheep represent people who follow God, then the shepherd would be God Himself." Roger looked up at him, and Marcus agreed.

"Who, then, is the one?"

Marcus's heart thumped in his chest, pushing all the air out of his lungs. "Someone who doesn't follow God," he said. *Like me*, he thought. *I am the lost sheep.*

He sat, breakfast forgotten, staring out the plate glass windows of the diner at the bright sunshine of the day. He was the lost sheep and God was pursuing Him. But why? It was crazy.

Roger finished off the last of his biscuits and gravy and picked up his coffee cup. Marcus drew in a deep breath and turned back to him. "Why now? I'm thirty-two years old. What's so special about now?"

Roger set his cup back down. "God's timing is a mystery we will never understand. But whatever the combination is of events, people, circumstances, readiness …it's what He has chosen. For you."

Marcus bit the corner of his lip between his teeth as he pondered this. "Hmm," was all he said but he picked up his fork and proceeded to polish off the pancakes. As he pushed his plate away, Roger spoke again.

"I owe you some more of my story," he said as he looked at his watch. "But I'm afraid we're out of time for today. How about next week?"

Marcus pulled out his wallet and put some bills on the table. "Is that your way of making sure I come back?"

"Whatever it takes."

Marcus studied the older man, amused. "Why not," he said as he put his wallet away. "It'll be your turn to buy."

13

All that week Corinne employed her new list, *Things to Do While Living in the Middle of Nowhere.* She'd sweated and stewed to fill it with activities she could complete in an evening, even starting from her little house in little Sutton and driving to someplace else. She found it wasn't so bad as long as she had her plans made ahead of time and could leave at five pm. An unexpected perk was that it gave her time to think and pray. She found it a nice opportunity to converse with God without dropping off to sleep like she often did at night.

One thing Corinne hadn't thought to start praying about was any potential romantic relationship she might be contemplating, consciously or unconsciously. She continued to frame that part of her life in terms of not getting distracted from her goals. So, she found her concentration wrecked the next Sunday when Marcus made an obvious point of sitting next to her in church. Before, she thought it just sort of happened.

Not that she minded sitting by him, but she could have smacked Daniel for the knowing look he had on his face. Thank goodness he was too far away to reach. Becky pretended like she hadn't seen a thing, which Corinne knew couldn't be true.

If the three of them already had some expectation of how things were going to turn out, then they were going to have problems. She had no intention of being railroaded into anything ever again. Couldn't they just be?

She was startled when the pastor stood up to preach. She hadn't heard a single thing in the service so far. So much for her prayers to not be distracted. *What's up with that, God? I prayed about it! Isn't that a good thing to pray for?* Annoyed with herself for not trying hard enough, she pulled out her phone and took notes to get herself back on track.

Thankfully it worked. After the benediction, she stood for a moment, lost in quiet contemplation over the message. She was startled from her reverie when Marcus gestured toward her phone and asked, "What do you do with all your notes?"

Corinne looked up at him. "Oh, nothing. It's just the act of note-taking. Helps me to focus."

"I get that. Lawyers do it all the time." Marcus's eyes crinkled as he smiled down at her.

Corinne's heart fluttered. She forgot how to breathe. And no wonder. That look was different from any she'd seen on his face before.

"Right?" was all she could choke out.

Becky grabbed her sleeve. "Hey, you coming?" Daniel motioned them forward, which reminded Corinne of her annoyance. She glanced down at the pew as she grabbed her bag in order to keep from glaring at him.

"Yeah, I'm coming." They greeted other worshippers as they moved toward the exit. Corinne was grateful for this distraction, because she was feeling quite grouchy again. *What the heck is the matter with me?*

It was a beautiful sunny day and that, combined with the open space and gentle breeze, served as a restorative for Corinne's good sense. *Thank goodness.* They stood in the parking lot, chatting amongst themselves, and then Corinne's mind wandered off to contemplate the quiet Sunday afternoon ahead of her, filled with all the mundane tasks necessary to life. She didn't mind them because stuff had to get done. It's just that today, on this beautiful sunny Sunday, she found herself wanting to spend time with her friends.

Seriously, what is wrong with me? Five minutes ago I was mad at all of them.

She was still wondering if she was losing her mind when she heard Becky exclaim, "I could stand out here in the sun all day! Except for the fact that I'm starving."

"Well, we'd better get some lunch then," Daniel said. "Where's it gonna be?"

"Home," Becky said. "We've got steaks to grill, remember?"

"Oh, yeah," Daniel said. "Almost forgot about that. And fresh vegetables to go with. Mmm mmm mmm, sounds delicious!"

Corinne's stomach grumbled. She couldn't help thinking how excellent a grilled steak sounded.

"You know, Daniel," Becky said. "I just realized we have four steaks out."

"You're right! Plus, that huge bag of farm-fresh vegetables. Not sure how you and I are going to eat it all. Oh, well. Leftovers, I guess."

"Oh, for the love of—" Marcus exclaimed. "You're both ridiculous!"

Daniel and Becky hooted and high-fived each other like a couple of kids. Corinne just watched and enjoyed. This was quintessential Daniel and Becky. *How fun it must be to have that in your life,* she thought. *Someone to laugh with.* She felt that pang again, the same one she'd had at the cookout.

Then her thoughts were interrupted by Becky, who had calmed down enough to ask, "Would you two like to join us for lunch?"

"Of course!" Marcus looked over at Corinne. "We're not passing up a steak dinner, are we?"

"No way!" Corinne agreed, thrilled with this turn of events, her mood swings forgotten. "But what can we bring?"

After a dash home to change out of her church clothes—but not into shorts—Corinne stopped by the store to pick up dessert. She would have rather taken something homemade, but the last-minute invitation didn't give her time. As she arrived at Daniel and Becky's, Marcus was getting out of his car with a cooler full of drinks. They walked up the steps together and Corinne rang the bell. Marcus gave her an appraising glance, which she happened to catch out of the corner of her eye. "What?"

He just shook his head, and before she could question him further, Daniel opened the door. "Perfect timing! I'm just about to fire up the grill." He and Marcus walked through the house and out to the back deck. Corinne stopped in the kitchen to help Becky prepare the vegetable skewers.

And that's all it took, that one simple activity of working together in the kitchen with Becky, for Corinne's changing perspective on life to lock into place. She looked back over the past six years and wondered, *How did I not realize what I was missing?* She spent the entirety of lunch basking in the joy of her newfound pleasure in friendship. It wasn't going to be perfect—as evidenced by her own grumpiness earlier—but somehow, it was still worth it.

It did not, however, mean that she was ready to trade in her old life completely. While the four of them lazed about on deck chairs after lunch, Daniel had a question for her.

"Where'd you go yesterday?"

"Cleveland."

"Alone?" Marcus asked.

"Of course, alone."

Marcus scoffed. "That's not fun."

"Says who?"

"Says me. Sightseeing is always more fun in a group."

"You know, he's got a point," Daniel said.

"Not if the group can't agree on what sights to see, or when, or for how long," Corinne countered.

"You know, she's got a point," Daniel said.

"Not a problem if you choose your group wisely." Marcus pinned her with his steady gaze.

"You know, he's got a point—"

Marcus said, "Dude! Shut up!"

Becky said, "Oh my word, Daniel!"

Corinne snorted. Then clapped her hand over her mouth and proceeded to giggle into it. Her eyes grew wide, and she doubled over, her shoulders shaking.

The other three sat in startled silence for the space of about two seconds. Then Daniel said, "You see? There's a woman who appreciates good humor!"

Corinne let out a little scream, and that set everybody off. For the next few moments, all conversation, intelligent or otherwise, ceased.

After everyone had calmed down, Marcus spoke up again. "Seriously, though, Corinne. Some places are better experienced with friends."

"Oh, I know," she replied. "I just like disagreeing with you." She smirked at him.

He gave her a look. "Of course you do."

"Well, I know one place that's better with friends, and I think we should all go," Becky said.

"Where's that?" Corinne wanted to know.

"Cedar Point."

"Oh, yeah! She's got a point—sorry. Sorry!" Daniel held up his hands in front of his face. "But she does. It would be awesome for the four of us to go to Cedar Point together. We haven't been there in a while."

"I've never been there," Corinne deadpanned.

"Ha, ha." That was Marcus. For the next several minutes he, Daniel, and Becky compared notes on their favorite coasters.

Corinne looked from one to the other as she listened. "So, when are we going?"

Within five minutes it was decided. A week from next Saturday, the foursome was headed to Cedar Point.

14

Marcus's thoughts about Corinne were racing all over the place as he lay in bed that night unable to sleep. On the one hand, spending the afternoon with Corinne was pure bliss. Bantering with her. Planning a whole day out together. It was perfect.

On the other hand, it was pure torment. She was so close to him, and yet so far away. Every time she squirmed in her chair, crossing and uncrossing her legs, he nearly hyperventilated.

Oh my god, those legs. It didn't matter that she wouldn't wear shorts again; he could imagine them. Marcus felt himself begin to harden and he shook his head sharply, trying to rid himself of the thoughts that would get him nowhere this night. It didn't help, so he threw off the covers and bounded out of bed over to the window, pressing his forehead to the screen in the hopes of catching a cool breeze.

No luck. He hustled into the bathroom and doused his head in the sink. Still not good enough. He got back in the shower, a cold one this time. He stood under the stream until his blood had cooled and the skin on his arms prickled with goosebumps.

That's when his thoughts turned in a surprising direction. It occurred to him that Corinne was purposefully choosing not to wear shorts around him. Which confused him. *What's the matter with shorts?* A lot of women left way less to the imagination with their clothing choices.

He toweled off and then slid between the sheets to lie there, fingers laced behind his head, thinking. Corinne was different in a lot of ways from the women he used to chase. *Which isn't a bad thing,* he acknowledged. In fact, most of it he found refreshing. Satisfying.

It also made it difficult, though, because he didn't seem to know how to proceed with her. Nothing worked the way he was used to. Marcus sighed and turned over, crushing the pillow in the crook of his arm. Not for the first time he wondered, *<u>why</u> is Corinne so different?*

"So let me get this straight," Marcus summarized the next morning at Maddie's. "You'd been out drinking the night before and woke up in your truck on some country road just in time to see a young woman slogging through the mud—because it rained overnight, and she had a flat tire—and you ended up marrying her."

"That's about the gist of it." Roger's eyes twinkled as he and Marcus finished their breakfast that Monday morning.

Marcus leaned back in his chair and shook his head. "How did you ever pull that one off?"

"Well, as you can imagine," Roger said, turning more serious as he sorted out a bite of hash browns with his fork. "I had a bit of straightening up to do. Nancy was on her way to worship that morning, you see. I offered to change the tire for her but what she wanted was a ride to church so she wouldn't be late." Roger paused, reliving the moment.

"When we got there, she said, 'I'd love for you to change the tire for me after church,' and she smiled." Roger shook his head. "I was done for. She could have asked anything of me. But she asked me to go to church with her, so I did."

Roger's eyes grew misty. "I didn't realize it at the time, but physically I was a complete mess that morning. It's a wonder they didn't throw me out. It's even more of a wonder that she felt safe being in my presence. But they didn't, and she did, and that was my first experience with church."

Marcus leaned forward and put his forearms on the table. "What happened next?"

Roger looked at his watch and sucked his breath in between his teeth. "Next time, my boy." He looked at Marcus, eyes twinkling again, and said, "And it'll be your turn to buy."

Marcus liked the practice of law, but he wasn't a workaholic. It's why he didn't stay in the city to vie for a spot in one of the 100-hour-a-week corporate firms like many of his classmates had. No, he was happy with just enough work to fill his weekdays, but not so much that it demanded his evenings and weekends, too.

That philosophy gave him the freedom to have a personal life. *Or at least to search for one,* he thought wryly. It also allowed him to enjoy things like having breakfast with Roger, an appointment he had come to look forward to each week, almost in spite of himself.

While he found himself amazed at Roger's story, he had no doubt about its veracity. He never would have guessed that this man who was so focused on God could have started out so messed up. *Like I am,* he thought uncomfortably.

That is to say, Marcus was beginning to suspect his life was messed up. He'd never thought so before. As far as he knew, it was normal, not any different from anyone else's. Recently, however, so many new ideas and people had presented themselves to him that he was no longer sure.

Thursday afternoon he had a follow-up meeting with Mrs. Fredrickson. Ms. Jackson, if she insisted, but not Abigail, whether she liked it or not. He had slipped up on that at the last meeting when he was distracted but made sure to fix it at this one. It was better not to get on a first name basis with his female clients. That could be a recipe for disaster.

This one, however, seemed to be all business, thank goodness. She had the financial documents he'd asked her to gather. Marcus perused them after she left, and everything seemed in order. Now he just needed to find an expert to review them for the case. Corinne came to mind and just like that, a new plan was formed.

Friday afternoon at 5:00 sharp, Marcus packed up the Fredrickson documents and left the office. He drove straight to Corinne's house only to find her car gone and the house quiet. *Again! That girl sure knows how to scram at the end of a workweek.* It was disappointing but not the end of the world. He'd try again tomorrow.

Early Saturday morning, Marcus grabbed the file and his car keys and headed out the door. He drove over to Corinne's house only to find her gone again. Or still; he wasn't sure which. "Seriously?" escaped his lips as he pulled to a stop in front of her house.

Why was it that he was having no luck meeting up with Corinne alone? Church was easy, and there had already been several social gatherings with Daniel and Becky, which was great. But all of those were group settings. What

Marcus wanted was a date, just the two of them, along with everything that implied.

He contemplated that pleasant thought as his car sat idling. But then he wondered, is that really what he wanted? Well, yes, of course it was, but it was just a few days ago that he had acknowledged differences in her. Did he want to handle her the same way he had every other woman?

The bigger question was, would he be able to help himself?

Oh, hell. He thumped the steering wheel in frustration. *Who knows?* Complicating matters was Roger and his story, getting all up in his thoughts. He tried to push away its similarity to his own, to convince himself it was just a coincidence. Roger was a nice man and Marcus liked talking with him. Corinne was a nice girl, and he was interested in her. Church had introduced him to both of them. That was great, but it didn't mean anything. A means to an end, that's all.

As Marcus drove back to his house, however, he was annoyed to discover that he had the same sense of unease as when he knew a client was feeding him a bunch of lies. Frustrated, off-kilter, and disappointed yet again, Marcus dropped off the Fredrickson file and headed out of town to visit his brother and his two nephews.

"Where have you been all weekend?" Marcus sniped as he slid into the pew next to Corinne on Sunday morning. She and Becky had been chatting.

Corinne turned toward Marcus, surprise written all over her features. "Excuse me?"

"You heard me." Marcus tilted his head back and looked down his nose at her.

Corinne arched her brows. "You're in a snit."

"Er, I beg your pardon. A snit?"

"Yes, a snit. What's the matter with you?"

Marcus looked away. "I just want to know where you were this weekend."

"And I guess you'll keep on wondering if that's how you're going to ask." She turned back to her friend. "Sorry about that, Becky. You were saying?"

From the other end of the pew, Daniel smirked at him. Had they been anywhere else, Marcus would have given him the finger. Instead, he just glowered as the two women resumed their conversation. He crossed his arms and tapped his foot, but they paid no further attention to him or his tantrum.

After a few moments, the music started, and the women ceased their conversation. Corinne took a deep breath and tilted her head upward to gaze at the ceiling. Then she bowed her head, exhaled, and closed her eyes.

This almost irritated Marcus. How could she be so calm when he was so unsettled? What was it about this place? He was off-balance here all the time and he didn't understand why.

As the service progressed, he managed to settle down, and by the time it ended, he regretted his snit. He turned to speak to Corinne right after the last amen, but Daniel and Becky were saying hurried goodbyes; they were headed out of town to visit Becky's parents. He had to wait his turn, again.

As soon as they were gone, he touched her arm. "Hey," he said. "I'm sorry. I didn't mean to be an ass. It just happens naturally, I guess."

Corinne's eyes sparkled with surprise, and she pressed her lips together. "I forgive you," she said. "And I'm sorry too."

"For what?" Marcus couldn't even imagine.

"I was being flippant, and I didn't realize you weren't until it was too late. Whatever your distress was, I'm sorry for adding to it."

Marcus was undone. She wasn't mad? He had expected an upbraiding, because women got mad at stuff like that, and stayed that way a long time. Instead, she'd said that phrase again. *I forgive you.*

Marcus tried to swallow the lump in his throat. "Thank you," he said.

"You're welcome," she replied. Then she added, "Hocking Hills."

Marcus blinked in surprise and then realized what she meant. "It's beautiful down there."

"It is." An awkward silence ensued, and she reached for her purse.

"I stopped by your house Friday evening," he said, before she could leave. "Saturday morning, too."

Corinne felt a tremor ripple through her body. "You did? I was gone."

Marcus raised an eyebrow. "I know."

There he was, the Marcus she knew and lo—. She stopped that thought in its tracks and instead asked, "Well, what did you want?"

"I wanted to ask you a business question. Can we sit?"

"Oh. Sure." Corinne dropped back into the pew and Marcus followed suit.

"I have a client," Marcus began, "a divorce case. There's a financial aspect to every divorce case of course, but this one is a little bit more involved. I need someone to review the documents and give an expert opinion on what's in them. I thought of you and wondered if you might be interested."

"Oh!" Corinne said again. "I've never done that before. For a legal case, I mean."

"It's not too big of a deal. We just need to make sure the numbers we've been presented with are adding up as they should."

Confusion touched Corinne's brow.

"What?" Marcus asked.

"Well, you could do that, couldn't you? I mean, you do know how to add, right?" She widened her eyes at him.

Marcus narrowed his. "What, don't you want the work?" He smirked at her and Corinne flicked her hand at him.

"Of course I do," she said. "But it sounds like a simple task. Not one that needs any particular expertise."

Marcus turned serious. "It's always better to get an expert opinion. Judges tend to frown upon lawyers who try to act as their own expert witnesses."

"Gotcha," she replied, understanding it better now. "Wait. Are you talking about courtroom testimony?"

"It shouldn't come to that."

"But...there's a possibility?"

Marcus hedged. "I guess there's always a possibility."

"Okay. It's just that I've never testified before."

"First time for everything." The amusement was back in his voice.

"That's true. It'd be a good experience to have, if it happened."

"That also is true," he agreed. "So, what do you say? You in?"

Pfft. Was he kidding? A new experience and a chance to work with him? No brainer!

"Yeah!" she said. "I am."

"One thing, though," Marcus added.

"What's that?"

"I'm going to need your contact information."

And just like that, he finally had her phone number.

15

Corinne scooted out pretty fast after their conversation. She had a ticket for a matinee theater performance in Columbus and she had to get on the road. She had decided it was better to make plans for this Sunday afternoon. Somehow, she thought it important to not always be available, no matter how much she enjoyed her friends' company. Now she was glad she had, because with Daniel and Becky headed out of town, this could have turned into the first time she and Marcus spent time alone together. Kind of like a date. She wasn't sure how she felt about that possibility.

As she headed straight out of town from the church, she pondered this. Was it just her being hesitant? *Or stubborn.*

Or did she sense something? *Maybe it was God's doing.* If so, why?

Corinne smacked the steering wheel. It was pointless to spend any more time arguing with herself about it. She had no answers. All she could say with any certainty at this point was that she was looking forward to the work he was bringing her. She refused to examine her reasons for this any further and instead turned the radio on full blast. She sang as loudly as she could to whatever songs she knew for the remainder of the drive. She was hoarse by the time she arrived.

She enjoyed the show, and her solitary dinner, and her drive home. It might not have been as much fun as grilling steaks had been last weekend, but it was still pleasant. The part for which she was most grateful was that it helped her to clear her head. When she went to work the next morning, she felt sensible and focused.

When Marcus contacted her by phone to set up a meeting date however, her struggles began anew. Corinne wasn't in the habit of meeting with clients in person. For one thing, they were scattered all over the country. For another, everything that needed to be done could be done virtually, and she preferred it that way.

But this was *Marcus*, and he was right here. It made sense to meet with him in person. Didn't it?

Oh dear.

When the day of the meeting arrived, Corinne was nervous. She took way more care than usual with her clothing selection. Usually, she dressed down for work. Even when she had video conferences, she could get away with more laid back choices. But not today. Not for an in-person meeting. It seemed to her that dressing for the part was important. Plus, she thought it might calm her nerves.

It must have worked, because Corinne's professionalism kicked in, and she focused her thoughts on the work as she finished getting ready. Just before she left the house, she said a brief prayer of thanks to God for the opportunity. Then she grabbed her keys and headed out the door.

The law firm was in a small upstairs suite in one of the many older buildings along Main Street. It wasn't large, nor did it need to be with just Marcus and his secretary. Irene worked in the front, just inside the main door. Marcus's office was down a small hallway behind her, with a break room and bathroom at the other end.

His office had all the items one would expect: shelves filled with books, storage cabinets, and a small conference table. It was tidy though; he didn't have stacks of files everywhere. Corinne felt oddly pleased by this.

What she hadn't expected was how dressed down Marcus was. He looked comfortable in his blue jeans and polo shirt. *Comfortable and quite appealing.* Corinne mentally slapped herself back to attention.

"Thanks for coming in," Marcus said as he showed her to a seat. He sat down behind his desk and gestured around the room. "Well, here it is. Not fancy but it gets the job done."

"That's all it takes," Corinne agreed.

Marcus went over issues of confidentiality and payment with Corinne. Once they had an agreement in place, he handed her a file with the financial documents in question and presented the basics of the case. Corinne skimmed the documents while he talked.

"I'd rather not say what it is we think you might find. I don't want to prejudice your review." Marcus looked up at her. "Just go over the documents, see what you can see, and we'll meet again to talk."

"Do you want a written report?"

"Yes, if you don't mind. That would be helpful."

And just like that, it was over. Brief, professional, efficient. Corinne was pleased, but also relieved. As cool as it was seeing Marcus in his work environment, she was glad to get back to her office. She loved working from home. It was so relaxed. First thing she did upon arriving was to trade out her meeting clothes for something more comfortable. Then she set to work reviewing the file. In the quiet, without an audience, she identified the discrepancies in the various reports. She spent the rest of the day making notes, preparing a spreadsheet to confirm her findings, and writing up a summary.

Just after 5:00 she set the file aside until her next meeting with Marcus. She went to bed that night feeling inordinately pleased with her day's work.

16

Friday at the end of the workday, Corinne sent a group text:

CP tomorrow? My house, 7am!

Next morning a bleary-eyed trio stumbled out of their cars and onto Corinne's postage stamp lawn. She, however, popped out of her house bright-eyed and ready to go.

"Why are you so perky this morning?" Becky lamented.

"For real," Daniel said. "It's 7:00 on a Saturday morning, for crying out loud!"

Marcus just yawned.

"Hey, you all are the ones who said we have to get there early to beat the traffic!" She widened her eyes at them in mock exasperation.

"Who's driving?" Marcus wanted to know.

"I am," Corinne replied.

Marcus rubbed his hands across his face. "I'd be glad to drive," he offered, and yawned again.

Corinne gave him a sideways glance. "No thanks; we want to get there alive." She inclined her head toward the car. "Let's go!"

Everybody piled in and fumbled with their seatbelts. Daniel and Becky snuggled into the back. Marcus stretched and settled in the front.

All her passengers were so quiet as they turned onto the highway a few minutes later that Corinne punched the radio to a Christian station and turned up the volume. That did the trick and soon everyone was wide awake. Daniel, Becky, and Corinne sang along with the radio wherever they knew the words. Marcus stared out the window as they did so but tapped his thigh in time to the rhythm.

They stopped for breakfast in Sandusky, and by the time they finished, the roads were filled with vehicles of people as eager as they were to spend the day in the park.

"I get why you could spend several days here," Corinne said. "We're going to be waiting in lines forever!"

"Lines are part of the fun!" Becky exclaimed.

"Only if you like the people you're in line with," Daniel quipped.

"Ha!" Corinne said. "Let's hope by the end of the day we all still like each other."

As they settled into their first line of the day, Daniel and Becky started chatting with some friends who were just ahead of them, leaving Marcus and Corinne standing side by side and shuffling forward together. After a minute, Marcus said, "Did you get a chance to go over the file?"

Corinne pointed her finger at him. "No business at the amusement park."

Marcus held up his hands in surrender. "Okay. What do you want to talk about?"

"Well, tell me something about yourself."

"What do you want to know?" His eyes sparkled as he looked down at her.

"Let's start with family. You mentioned nephews at the cookout."

"Yep, my brother's kids. Two of them, 16 and 14. Both playing football. You?"

"One sister. She and her husband have two little ones with another on the way." They moved forward a couple of steps in line. Corinne then asked, "Have you always lived in Ohio?"

Marcus nodded. "Went to college here, too."

"I did the same thing in Indiana. In fact, I went to college in my hometown. Everybody thought I was crazy."

"Well, did you like it?"

"I did. I liked the school, and I liked being near my family."

"Worth it then. Good family, I take it?"

She shrugged. "Not perfect, but nobody's is. You?"

"Eh, not so much."

Corinne grimaced. "Sorry." She was curious to know more but hesitant to ask. Instead, she chose this question: "How did you decide on law school?"

"Let's just say I was always in trouble for arguing with my teachers. I was a smart-aleck, know-it-all kid." He gave her a look to ward off any smart-aleck response, and Corinne pressed her lips together to keep one from escaping.

"It was during one of my many trips to the principal's office; I think he was fed up with my arguing, and he said, 'Marcus, you're going to be a great lawyer someday.' It kind of stuck."

She contemplated his answer as they continued to move forward. "That's cool, though. It just goes to show we never know when something we say is going to have an impact on somebody's life."

Marcus raised his eyebrows. "I guess." They were both quiet for a few moments, then Marcus said, "What about you and all those places you've lived? Didn't you ever want to stay in any of them?"

"I mean, there were some great places, but I always reached the point where I felt like—" she hesitated and looked across the midway. "Like it was time to move on." When she turned back, she found Marcus studying her.

"Never met anybody who made you want to stay?"

Corinne pursed her lips and shook her head.

Marcus raised an eyebrow. "Seriously, in all that time?"

"Seriously." She turned away to lean on the railing, putting an end to the line of questioning. Her experience in college hadn't left her eager to try again, but neither had she met anyone since who made her want to. How hard was it to find a guy that was both nice, and a Christian, at the same time? And how could you explain that to someone you might be interested in?

Marcus leaned on the railing next to her. When she looked over at him, she found him watching her, an amused look on his face.

"What?" she asked.

"Nothing. Just curious what you're thinking."

Corinne didn't respond. Thankfully she didn't have to, because Daniel and Becky started a good-natured argument about how many ride sessions they still had to wait. "There is no way it's still twenty runs away from our turn!"

This was Daniel. "Dude, tell her!" he said to Marcus. Marcus just held up his hands.

"Whatever, Daniel," Becky retorted. "We'll see who's right when we reach the front of the line." She made a face at him and then pulled Corinne up next to her. "Do not make me talk to my husband all day long!" she whispered. Corinne snickered behind her hand.

She and Becky chatted together for the rest of the wait. Daniel and Marcus did the same, and nobody bothered to count the rides until they reached the front. When they got there, Becky joined her husband in a cart, leaving Marcus and Corinne to sit together in the next one. For a brief moment, Corinne felt awkward. Then she shook it off.

All good, she told herself. *You wouldn't want it any other way, would you?* She relished this private conversation with herself as she tightened the safety harness. *Of course not.*

"All good?" Marcus asked.

Corinne almost choked over his choice of words. She regained control of herself and then looked up at him. "Yep!"

"What?"

She raised her eyebrows. "Nothing." Then the roller coaster took off and all conversation ended.

With seating partners and walking buddies sorted out, the rest of the morning flew by without any more awkwardness. Corinne was having a blast.

At lunch, they grabbed burgers and fries and sat down at an outdoor table. "What ride do you want to hit next, Corinne?" Becky asked, dipping a fry into her ketchup.

"Hey, I'm good with any of them."

"Let's do the Dragster then," Daniel said.

"Great idea," Marcus replied. "And we should go see a show tonight."

"Ooh, that sounds like fun!" Becky grabbed a park brochure and she and Corinne bent their heads together to figure out the best place to go for that.

Later, as they waited in line for the Top Thrill Dragster, Corinne and Becky chattered together while Daniel and Marcus debated the structural merits of the ride they were waiting in line for.

"Are you serious, Daniel?" Becky widened her eyes at her husband. "We're getting ready to ride on that thing!" The guys just sniggered.

They watched group after group take their turns experiencing the thrill of the ride. Daniel turned to his wife and said, "Looks like it's working great." Becky huffed and Daniel gave her a little squeeze. "We'll be fine."

When they reached the front of the line, Marcus and Corinne climbed into their seats and pulled down the restraining bars. Corinne wriggled in anticipation and Marcus looked at her out of the corner of his eye. "Nervous?"

"Pfft, no." The cart inched forward and stopped at the light bar. It seemed an eternity before they jerked forward, hurtling down the track. They shot 420 feet straight up into the air, twisted over the summit, and spiraled their way back down to earth at 120 miles per hour, whooping and hollering the entire way. Seventeen seconds of pure adrenaline.

As they came to a stop, Corinne leaned her head back and laughed in sheer delight. "That was awesome!" Marcus helped her out of the cart. They joined Daniel and Becky as they exited the ride.

"Best ride ever!" Corinne exclaimed.

"Yeah," Daniel said. "It's a great return on investment. Two hours in line for a twenty second ride!"

"Oh my gosh, Daniel!" Becky smacked him on the arm. "It's all part of the fun! Besides, the Dragster was your idea!" Daniel raised his hands while Corinne and Marcus snickered at their antics.

The early July weather was mild and a bit overcast. It made standing in lines surrounded by hundreds of people bearable. It also made Corinne forget to drink water, which wasn't a problem until dinnertime. They opted for an indoor restaurant and enjoyed salad and breadsticks as they waited for their entrees.

Corinne ordered pasta with sausage, peppers, and onions. She was just a few bites in when she realized her mistake. "Oh, no," she whispered and dropped her fork.

Becky glanced up. "What's the matter?"

"I shouldn't have ordered this," Corinne said and pushed her plate away.

"What's wrong with it?" Marcus asked.

"Nothing. The sausage."

"Is it bad?" Daniel wanted to know.

"No, it's the preservatives. Sometimes they make me sick." Corinne grabbed her glass and gulped the contents. "I need more water."

Marcus scanned the restaurant and signaled their server. "Could you bring some more water? Hurry." The waitress rushed off, sensing the urgency of the request.

The corkscrews of pain had already begun in the middle of Corinne's back. The tightness crawled upward and outward, winding its way across her shoulder blades and into her neck. She squirmed in her chair and stretched her arms, trying desperately to relieve it.

As soon as the server returned and filled her glass, Corinne drained it. But it was too late. Her head was already gripped in a vice. "I need some pain medicine." She and Becky both reached for their bags. Corinne found hers first, as she always carried it with her. She poured three tablets into her hand, and then realized her glass was empty again.

"I need more water." Her tongue was beginning to feel thick.

Marcus jumped up. "I'll get it."

"Do—do you want to order something else?" Daniel asked, but Corinne just shook her head. Becky's face was tense as she looked over at her husband.

Corinne shifted in her seat. "Where's the water?"

"It's right here." Marcus was back. He filled her glass and set a pitcher on the table, watching as she swallowed the medicine and more water.

Corinne then leaned back in her chair. "Don't let your food get cold."

Daniel picked up his fork, but didn't eat anything. Becky just kept staring.

Marcus inhaled and then said, "Maybe we should go." He looked across at Daniel, who nodded his agreement.

"Uh-uh." Corinne closed her eyes and rubbed the back of her neck. "I just need time."

The other three finished as quickly as they could, and then they left the restaurant. They made their way back toward the midway, but the light-hearted atmosphere was gone. When they came upon a shaded area with picnic tables, Corinne headed toward them.

"I'm going to sit." She slumped down on a bench. "You guys come back later."

"I am not leaving you here alone." Marcus turned to Daniel and Becky. "You two go on and I'll stay here with Corinne."

Reluctantly, Daniel and Becky moved off toward the midway and Marcus sat down next to Corinne. She squirmed and shifted about. There were no comfortable positions. As she squeezed first one shoulder and then the other, Marcus asked, "Would it help if I massaged?"

"Oh, would you?" Her face was drawn, her eyes filled with pain.

Marcus turned sideways on the bench and then guided her by the shoulders to face away from him. He was hesitant at first, his touch tentative, but gradually he applied more pressure. "Wow, your muscles are so knotted."

"Mmm," she murmured and closed her eyes.

Marcus worked for a long time, kneading out the tension in her shoulders, her upper back, and her neck. When the muscles started to relax, Corinne dropped her head forward. He leaned around to look in her face. "Better?"

"Much better. Thank you." Then she turned toward the table, laid her head on her arms, and fell asleep.

When she awoke about twenty minutes later, her eyes were dull and her brain foggy. She felt like a sloth, but the pain was no longer building. She turned and looked at Marcus, who was watching her. "Hey," she said and stretched.

"How are you feeling?"

"I'll live." She turned around to face out from the picnic table, and Marcus did the same.

"When Daniel and Becky get back, I think we should head home," he said.

Corinne shook her head. "I want to see the show." She yawned.

Marcus frowned but said nothing more. When Daniel and Becky returned, they were relieved to see her on the mend, but they too thought they should head home.

Corinne shook her head. "I've got the car keys." She chuckled weakly.

Marcus tipped his head toward her and raised an eyebrow. "You are stubborn."

She closed her eyes. "Which way to the show?"

Daniel and Becky pulled out the map to get their bearings and then they all headed off through the crowd. They found a spot with four seats together and settled in, Marcus on one side of Corinne and Becky on the other, with Daniel watching over his wife's shoulder.

They all kept a close eye on Corinne, who was still lethargic. At one point she looked around at them and said, "I'm okay. I just have to deal with the fallout now."

Marcus huffed.

"And you helped me a lot with that massage," she said. "Sometimes it's the only thing that keeps it from getting full-blown."

Becky's eyes widened. "That wasn't full-blown?"

Corinne closed hers. "Not even close." Daniel whistled and shook his head.

When the show ended, they got up and moved along with the crowd toward the parking lot. Corinne fumbled in her bag until she came up with the keys, which she silently handed to Marcus. He pocketed them, then took her arm and folded it around his own. Daniel took hold of his wife's hand and led the way.

It was as slow of a process getting out of Cedar Point as it had been getting in. Long before they hit the main road, Corinne was out, and she only woke up when they pulled into her driveway.

"Oh, wow." She stretched and yawned as they all gathered their belongings and got out of the car. "I'm sorry."

"Don't be silly," Becky said and then gave her a big hug. "You gonna be okay?"

Corinne quirked her mouth in a half smile. "Yeah. I'll be fine."

Daniel and Becky went straight to their car and left, but Marcus walked Corinne to the door. "You sure?"

"I'm sure." She looked up at him. "Thank you for everything."

"You're welcome." His eyes were warm and serious.

Corinne turned away. "I should go in."

"Of course." He retrieved the keys, turned them in the lock, and then handed them over. "Goodnight, Corinne."

"Goodnight, Marcus."

Corinne went inside and shut the door.

17

Next morning Marcus hit the alarm and turned over on his back. *No way Corinne will be in church today,* he thought. He threw his arm over his head and went back to sleep.

Or tried to. Instead, he tossed and turned for half an hour and then gave up. With a bit of hustle, he could have made it to the service, but the thought never even crossed his mind. He showered and shaved, then got dressed and ate breakfast. After that he wandered around the house for the rest of the morning, not sure what to do with himself.

What did I used to do on Sunday mornings, he wondered? *Sleep, that's what*. Usually because he'd been out half the night. It surprised him to think how long it had been since he'd done that—and how he didn't miss it.

That afternoon, as early as he thought reasonable, he drove over to Corinne's. She was reading on the porch, sitting in one of two brand new deck chairs, a fact which he found amusing.

"Hey," he called out as he came up the walk. "How are you feeling?"

She laid the book in her lap. "Getting there."

He took a seat in the second chair and scrutinized her. "That was terrible."

"Tell me about it."

"You shouldn't do that to yourself."

Corinne threw up her hands. "I know, but sometimes I forget."

"Hmm." Marcus was still feeling protective of her and her casual attitude about the whole episode confused him. *Why even risk it, as sick as it made her after only a few bites?*

Down the street, a group of young children were squealing with delight as they cooled themselves in a sprinkler.

Marcus watched them for a few moments and then looked back at Corinne. "What are you reading?"

She held it up. "*Waves of Mercy* by Lynn Austin."

"Never heard of it."

"It's about Dutch Christians who immigrated to Michigan in the mid-1800s, so they could have the freedom to worship as they thought best." She rubbed her hand across the cover of the book. "I can't even imagine. We take it for granted."

Marcus recalled a similar statement Roger had made early in their acquaintance. He was still pondering this when Corinne spoke again. "Speaking of worship. We missed you this morning. You were the only lazy bones of the bunch."

Marcus blanched. "You went to church?"

Corinne nodded.

"I didn't think you'd be there."

"It was just a headache, and the pain was gone before I went to bed last night."

Of course she was there. This is the woman who walked eight blocks to get to church when she had a flat tire. Marcus mentally kicked himself. "Well, I'm sorry I missed you."

Corinne shot him a glance. "What do you mean?"

"If I'd known you were going to be there, I would have come."

At these words, Corinne's facial expression changed. Her eyes darkened and she furrowed her brow. "Hold on," she said and stared at him. Marcus quaked under this sudden change in her demeanor. "Have you been going to church because of me?"

"Well, yeah. It was the only way I could meet you. Dan wouldn't tell me your name unless I did. He invites me all the time, but I never—"

He stopped. He couldn't interpret the look on her face. It looked like surprise, but there was something else mixed in. Something that made him break out in a sweat.

Corinne looked away toward the children down the street, and the silence stretched between them. The longer it went on, the more nervous Marcus became. This piece of information was apparently significant, but how or why he had no idea. So, he just sat and waited, at a complete loss for what to do next.

Corinne was quiet for a long time. When she finally turned back to look at him, she said, "So, how's it been?"

Startled, he fumbled. "How's it—what do you mean? You mean church?"

She nodded.

Marcus opened his mouth to reply, but nothing came out. *How had it been? Confusing, disconcerting, troubling at times.* "Honestly, it's kind of turned my world upside down."

To his great surprise, Corinne smiled—but only with her lips. "The thing is, Marcus, when God gets ahold of us, that's what happens. And He uses all kinds of ways to get our attention." She stopped and peered up at the sky, deep in thought. "You know what I think?" Without waiting for an answer, she continued. "You say you *came* to church to meet me. But I think God *brought* you to church to meet Him."

Marcus said nothing. How could you respond to such a thing? When the silence grew long and uncomfortable once again, he begged off, citing his desire to let her rest. Corinne didn't argue. She just said, "Okay. See ya."

"Yeah. See ya."

It was a long afternoon and an even longer night in his big, quiet, lonely house. The one saving grace was that the next day was Monday and he could talk with Roger. *Thank God for Roger*, he thought, and then wondered at himself for thinking it.

Apparently, Roger could read him like a book, because as soon as Marcus walked through the door, he took one look at him, ushered him to a table, and said, "Tell me about your weekend, Marcus."

For his part Marcus was thinking he should quit being surprised by anything that happened with his new church friends.

He was comfortable enough with Roger by this point, however, that he had no qualms telling him about their day at Cedar Point and his conversation with Corinne on Sunday afternoon. "One minute I think everything's headed in just the right direction, and the next, it's all shot to hell. Ahh, sorry." He rubbed his hands over his face and through his hair. Then he flipped his hand in the air. "At least, I think it is. I don't know." He looked up at Roger. "What's wrong with me?"

Roger's eyes crinkled as he smiled. "Not a thing. God has a way of getting under our skin when He's trying to get our attention."

"So, you think that's what this is, too."

Roger pursed his lips. "What do you think, Marcus?"

Marcus blew out his breath. "No idea."

"Well, put your lawyer brain to work. Let's look at the evidence."

Something clicked in Marcus's head. "Okay."

"When did everything go off-kilter?"

"When I met—" Marcus stopped and scrutinized his thoughts. "No, that's not it. It was the second Sunday I went to church. When we had that dinner. That's when I first started hearing...surprising things."

"Who was saying these surprising things?"

"Well, you for one. And Corinne. Later on, the pastor, when I started listening to him, I mean." Marcus couldn't count the number of times he'd made that very same confession to Roger.

Roger seemed not the least bit troubled by it, though. "And what is the nature of these surprising things that people are saying?"

"Well, for example, you reference God in pretty much everything you say. That's not the kind of conversation I'm used to hearing." Marcus thought some more. "Corinne, she gets involved during worship. She takes notes, for crying out loud, and will walk eight blocks to be there." His shoulders slumped, and he added, "She'll go even when she's been sick with a headache."

"So, God is central in the statements and behaviors you find surprising?" Roger asked.

"Yeah, I guess so."

"What about your friends, Daniel and Becky?"

"What about them?"

"Are they saying surprising things?"

"No. They're the same as they've always been."

"Do they speak of God?"

Marcus thought long and hard about this. Daniel had been inviting him to church for years, invitations which Marcus had always declined. Daniel always bowed his head before a meal, even at Maddie's on Fridays, a habit Marcus had paid little attention to in the past.

But now that the question had been asked, Marcus began to realize that everything Daniel and Becky did, both together and separately, was different from how the other people in his life behaved. Different from his family, different from people on the social scene, different from clients.

Now he was meeting other people like Daniel and Becky, and what they all had in common was God. Marcus looked up at Roger in surprise. "Everything they do speaks of God." He shook his head in disbelief. "How did I miss that?"

"It's not that you missed it, but rather that God has now opened your eyes to it," Roger explained.

Marcus sat deep in thought for a few moments. He still didn't understand why God was chasing him down. He was also confused about how he could have been so blind to what was, apparently, all around him. The explanation that God was opening his eyes didn't make sense in the world Marcus knew.

Unfortunately, their time was up for this day, so he dragged himself off to work after breakfast with more questions than he'd had when they started—and no conclusions about where he stood with Corinne.

18

Corinne slapped her computer shut. She'd been staring at it all that Monday morning but accomplishing little. She still couldn't believe it. Marcus wasn't a Christian. She closed her eyes and shook her head. How had she missed that?

How on earth had she missed all the signs? They were clear as day now: his confusion over communion, not being familiar with the potluck dinners, his surprise when she forgave him. Shaking her head, she dragged herself off to the kitchen for an early lunch, even though she wasn't hungry.

She had tried to be cautious. Warned herself to be cautious. Even prayed about it, for crying out loud! But somewhere along the way, she had failed. Somewhere along the way she'd let herself get interested in this guy way too soon.

Because she was definitely interested, in spite of it all. Corinne liked Marcus.

There. She admitted it. She liked him.

She had let herself fall for him. And she knew better. If her history had given her anything, it was the wisdom not to get too interested too soon.

She pulled stuff out of the refrigerator to make a sandwich. Where had she gone wrong? Had she spent too much time with her new friends? Not prayed enough?

She paused, her knife hovering over the jar of mayonnaise. Had she prayed wrong? She'd asked to not get distracted and that she be careful. Didn't that cover it? Had she not been specific enough? She finished making her sandwich and ate it while the unanswered questions continued to swirl in her brain.

Including the question of how to get out of the situation. Here she was, stuck in a tiny town with a small circle of friends that included him. You couldn't just disappear in a place like this, not like you could in the city.

Thing was, she didn't want to disappear. She liked it here. There. She admitted that, too.

After lunch, she went back to her desk, but she didn't open her work software. Instead, she texted Evelyn to see if she was available to video chat. To her great relief, she was. Corinne poured out her story, ending with her concern about possibly having to move again.

Evelyn was silent for a moment, processing everything Corinne had just told her. Then she drew in a deep breath and said, "Last time we talked, you shared with me that you felt God's call on you there in Sutton, to share Christ with others through your daily life. How does that fit in with all this?"

"I don't know." She thought for a moment. "I suppose a person can live their life for Christ from anywhere."

"Yes," Evelyn replied, "but from all you've told me, it was your arrival in Sutton that served as a catalyst for Marcus to begin learning about God."

Corinne frowned. "That doesn't have to stop just because I leave."

"You think he'll continue going to church if you're not there?"

"What are you saying? That I have to stay here *because* of him? I can't witness to him with an ulterior motive!"

"You're right about that. You cannot. But that's your burden to bear, not his. If he truly is seeking, you don't want to do anything to discourage that." When Corinne huffed, Evelyn asked point blank. "Which is more important, your discomfort or his salvation?"

Corinne dropped her forehead into the palm of her hand. "His salvation. Of course."

"Exactly. And that is what should guide your decisions." Her voice became gentle. "Whether God brought you here or you chose it, I don't know. But either way, He is at work. Let Him work." She pointed skyward. "You just keep your focus on Him."

It did make sense. A little anyway. "How do I do that?" Corinne asked. "I was praying, or I thought I was. What else can I do to keep from..." Corinne's voice trailed off, and she raised her hands helplessly.

"Just as always, read the Word and stay in worship. And keep praying, but not just for yourself and your path, but for Marcus, too. For his journey toward faith." Evelyn thought for a moment. "One time I heard a preacher say that the best way to deal with attraction, whether appropriate or inappropriate, is to pray for the person you're attracted to. It places them in God's hands and puts you in closer communion with God."

Corinne was silent as the realization struck her. She hadn't prayed for Marcus. She'd only prayed for herself. It was only recently that she'd begun praying for Daniel and Becky, and as crazy as it sounded, it was a new thing for her. Outside of "God bless's" for her family, and the litany of "please heal's" that were ever-present in church prayers, Corinne had never prayed for others in earnest. For their lives. Their salvation.

How had she missed that, too?

"Ask God to guide you, Corinne, in all things. Don't run from the life He has allowed you to inhabit just because it feels uncomfortable. Let Him lead, and you follow. I'll be praying for you."

19

It was a long week for Marcus. He felt like he was waiting, but for what, he wasn't sure. Mostly he just wanted to know where he stood with Corinne. Had he been dismissed from her life? If so, why? Because he was in church to meet her? *That should have been flattering,* he thought.

Maybe she didn't think so.

Not knowing the answers to any of those questions left Marcus to make his own assumptions, none of which were pleasant.

Of course, he could have reached out to her. He had her phone number. But he didn't do it. The reality was that Marcus's experience in life so far, even from childhood, was that things worked out for a while, and then they didn't. And you moved on. It's the pattern he learned from his family and the one he employed in his life.

It's how the world works, he thought. He saw it in his business. Marriage failed? Get divorced. Business partnership gets tough? Part ways. That's how people lived their lives.

Except for—Marcus stopped. He recalled his most recent conversation with Roger about Daniel and Becky and how everything they did spoke of God. They were still together. And Roger and his wife had been married for decades. They were all part of this church world, the one that Marcus found so confusing. Apparently, they didn't just move on when things got tough. Was that why?

More questions with no answers.

The one thought that did bring him a measure of comfort—instead of discomfort, like it usually did—was that Corinne was also part of that church world. He hoped it would mean that she wouldn't just give up on him. Because contrary to every thought he'd just had, every choice he'd ever made in his life otherwise, he didn't want to move on from Corinne. He liked her. As in, really liked her.

It brought a small spark of hope, but it wasn't enough move him to action. He didn't reach out. He didn't know how. Instead, he burrowed in, canceling basketball, begging off lunch, and rescheduling meetings. The result was that by Sunday morning he was agitated and impatient.

When his alarm rang that morning, he slapped at it, swung his legs over the edge of the bed, and sat up. *A day of reckoning,* he thought. Today he'd find out where he stood with Corinne, if there was any chance with her, or not. He stared out the window at a world oblivious to his distress. When he could have used a little commiseration, all he received was indifference.

He arrived early and stood at the back of the sanctuary, shifting his stance every few moments and tapping his fingers against his thighs as he glanced about the room and waited. For all his vigilance, Corinne managed to slip in beside him unseen.

"Good morning, Marcus." Marcus flinched and spun to face her. "It's good to see you here," she said, her eyes serious. She offered a small smile and then, without waiting for an answer, moved off to talk with one of the ladies who'd been at the cookout.

Marcus just stared after her. He couldn't move, couldn't think. He was still in this state when Daniel and Becky arrived. Becky joined the group of women and Daniel sidled up beside his friend. "Thought maybe you'd dropped off the planet."

Marcus bobbed his head to the side. "Almost."

Before Daniel could respond, the pastor was calling everyone to take their seats. Marcus ended up back in his original spot next to Daniel, instead of next to Corinne. He couldn't decide if it was a relief or a torment, so he tried to put it out of his mind and focus on the service. He was surprised that the service brought a bit of comfort to him. He hadn't expected that.

Afterward, the four of them exited the building, chatting together as they went. Actually, it was only three of them who were chatting; Marcus was still quiet. He was waiting for an opportunity to speak with Corinne privately. She didn't linger though; she had plans and had to get going.

Of course she had plans. She always had plans. Could the girl not stay still for one minute?

As she was about to take her leave, he found his voice and stopped her. "Hey, Corinne, hold up. I was wondering if we could schedule that meeting to go over your findings on the Fredrickson case."

"Sure. What works for you?"

After consulting their calendars, they settled on Tuesday morning at 11:00.

"That sounds good. I'll see you then." She turned to Daniel and Becky. "Bye, guys! I'll catch up with you sometime this week." With a breezy wave she headed to her car and was gone. And Marcus still had no answers.

At least not complete answers. She hadn't ignored him, but she hadn't talked with him, either. Not really. He glowered over his inability to make happen the conversation that he so desperately needed to have.

"Marcus, hello?" This was Becky.

"Dude, you there?" That was Daniel.

They had been trying to get his attention. "Sorry. What do you need?"

"Wondered if you want to come to lunch. Becky's got lasagna and all the fixings."

"Sure. That sounds great." *Why not,* he thought. He had no desire to be in solitary confinement with his own thoughts any longer.

Unfortunately, the company didn't do much to help, so rather than growl at his friends, he excused himself soon after they ate and retreated to his home anyway. By the time Monday morning breakfast rolled around, his mood was even worse.

It's a good thing Roger was a wise and discerning man. As such he obliged Marcus's rather gruff request for another installment of his own story rather than any discussion about Marcus's life. This brought another small bit of comfort to Marcus, a respite from his thoughts. Plus it was entertaining. For these things he was grateful. What it didn't do, however, was resolve anything. Marcus didn't see how Roger could help him do that anyway. He had to talk to Corinne.

He spent the rest of the day with his office door closed, taking no calls and accomplishing the barest minimum of work. Mostly he was obsessing over tomorrow's meeting with Corinne. He prowled around his house all evening and tossed and turned all night.

Tuesday morning he was wound as tight as he'd ever been. But he was determined they would have it out, once and for all, no matter what.

20

Corinne had gone home from church to her quiet little house, stood a moment in the doorway, and then headed in to change clothes. She grabbed her bag and the lunch she'd packed that morning, and left town.

She'd thought it best to have plans for after church again.

It hadn't gone badly, not by a long shot, but she certainly wasn't ready to test herself by socializing together. Not yet. So, she had planned this trip to spend the afternoon outdoors down at Mohican.

It was a gorgeous day and ended up being the perfect restorative. She walked the trails where she met occasional groups of people. She even did some canoeing. The sun, the quiet, and the need to pay attention to what she was doing out on the water gave her a wonderful respite from her cares.

It was with a renewed sense of purpose that she prayed that night. "Lord, even though I'd like to have all the answers, I know You don't work that way. So, I'm lifting it all up to You. This place where you've brought me. These people You've allowed me to meet." She prayed specifically for Daniel and Becky and their longing for children. Then she prayed for Marcus.

"The most important thing is his salvation. I know this. So, I'm asking, whatever interaction You allow us to have, let it be for his eternal good. Surround him with people who will share Your love with him." She hesitated, uncertain about this next part. "Bless him, Father, but not so much that he's comfortable without You." She worried a little about that prayer. "You know what I mean, right God?" Corinne had never prayed for anyone's salvation before. How did you ask for whatever it would take for someone to recognize their need for God?

As she ground through the days and hours before her meeting, every time she felt a sense of anxiety she turned it over to God in prayer. She found herself praying a lot between Sunday evening and Tuesday morning.

She was grateful to have had a good night's sleep on Monday. The next morning, she showered and dressed professionally once again. She still thought it was the right thing to do, but now she realized it was staying in prayer that mattered most. Shortly before eleven, she grabbed her keys and the file and left the house. She prayed the entire short drive. Not about the topic; that didn't worry her at all. It was the other stuff. *Help me to represent You well, Father,* she prayed as she drove downtown. *Help me to be at peace and to stay focused on You. Amen.*

Irene greeted her and showed her back to Marcus's office. "Good morning!" she said brightly, even though her insides were quaking.

"Morning. I hope you've got some good news for me."

Corinne raised her eyebrows. *All business. Okay then.* "We'll see," she replied.

They took their seats at a small worktable in Marcus's office and got right to work. Corinne went over the documents and her report, with Marcus following along.

When she finished, he said, "This is fantastic! And you're sure about these findings?"

"Yes, if you look here, at this column of numbers and compare them with these," she pointed to one of the original documents, "you can see there are thousands of dollars unaccounted for."

Marcus leaned back and rubbed his hands together. "Ms. Jackson," he said, putting great emphasis on the name, "is going to be thrilled. Her husband is dead meat." Something like a growl came from deep in his throat. Corinne was startled, and then she saw the look on his face. It was one she'd never seen before.

"You look like you're enjoying this," she said.

"Absolutely. People behave badly in marriage and pay the price in divorce."

Corinne bounced her leg up and down as she considered this. "Not everyone does."

"Most do." Then added under his breath, "I should know."

But not soft enough; she heard him. "What do you mean?"

His eyes were dark. "I know about people behaving badly in marriage."

Corinne frowned. "Well, sure, because you're a divorce lawyer. That's the side of people you see."

Marcus stared at her, his lips pressed into a thin line. "Not exactly." His eyes were devoid of the usual teasing sparkle and warm friendliness that made them so irresistible.

Corinne had moved beyond startled. This didn't look like Marcus at all. In fact, it wasn't the look of someone she would normally be comfortable being alone with, yet here she was. "What do you mean?" she said again.

"What I mean," Marcus said, enunciating each word, "is that I have personal experience on the subject."

Corinne blinked in surprise. "You've been divorced?"

Marcus nodded one time, never taking his eyes off hers.

Corinne lifted her gaze to the window as she absorbed this news. Her thoughts were in a complete scramble. What came out of her mouth was, "It must have been horrible to make you feel that way."

Marcus snorted and shot out of his chair. He stalked to the window and stared out. After a moment, he turned and leaned against the sill, crossing his arms in front of his chest.

"Yes, it was," he said in a clipped tone. "Both times."

Corinne heard the words. She did. But as they registered, her vision narrowed to a single point. Her ears filled with the sound of her beating heart. Everything else in the entire world ceased to exist. She struggled even to breathe.

She had no idea how long she was in that state, but when the world came back online, she found Marcus staring at her, his face a terrible mixture of defiance and something else. *What was it?*

She swallowed hard. "You're saying that you've been married and divorced twice."

Marcus blew out his breath. "Yes, Corinne, that's what I'm saying."

Corinne nodded and looked away, staring at the shelf full of dark volumes on the other side of the table. Her entire body was quivering now, but her mind was still frozen.

Marcus turned back to the window and shoved his hands in his pockets. Neither of them spoke for several minutes.

When the shock began to dissipate and Corinne's brain started to function again, she took a deep shuddering breath and blew it out. Then, almost without thinking, she offered up a prayer in her mind. *Your words, Father.* At once she opened her mouth to speak, but again without knowing what those words would be. "Have you ever thought—"

"What? That I'm the problem?" Marcus whipped around. "Like I've never heard that one before." He grabbed the stack of papers off the table and retreated to stand behind his desk.

This outburst had the strange effect of calming Corinne. She turned in her seat to face him. "Not quite what I was going to say."

"No?" Marcus busied himself tapping the edges of the papers together into a neat pile.

"No," she said and then just waited.

Marcus threw the papers down, scattering them across the surface of his desk. "What then?" He glared at her, throwing out his hands and letting them fall against his sides.

Corinne held his gaze. "I was just wondering if you had considered that marriage might not be the solution to whatever the problem is."

His defiance crumbled before her eyes. Defiance and—*What was it?* She wasn't sure. Marcus gaped at her for a few moments and then dropped into his chair, staring off into the distance.

"What do you think the problem is?" he asked in a small voice, not daring to look at her.

"It's the same one we all have."

He turned to face her then, brows lowered, eyes guarded. "What's that?"

"We each have a hole in our heart we're trying to fill. We try everything. Relationships." She gestured toward him. "Money." She waved her hand at the stack of papers. She thought for a moment and then tapped her own chest. "Change." She studied her fingernails as she contemplated that last one.

Then she shook her head. "None of those things will fill it. Only one thing can, only one Being."

Marcus inhaled. "I suppose you mean God."

"Yes." Corinne turned back to him. "Only God is able to fill the hearts that He creates."

Marcus reached out a single hand and fiddled with the edge of one of the papers on his desk. Then without looking up, he said, "Thanks for your work on this project."

Corinne was silent for a few moments and then replied, "You're welcome." She gathered her things and left the room.

She stumbled down the stairs and out the door and to her car. She struggled to unlock it as her hands shook. Once inside she threw down her purse and slumped into the driver's seat.

Did I say goodbye to Irene? I can't remember. What else do I have to work on today? I hope there's no more meetings. Do I have anything for lunch in the fridge? I should call Mom, see how she's doing. She pounded the palm of her hand against her forehead, willing her brain back to orderliness. She pushed the key into the ignition, started the car, and drove away.

A few minutes later she pulled into her driveway and just sat. Shock had given way to extreme weariness, and Corinne wasn't sure she could muster the strength to open her car door. Then she decided not to. She put the car in reverse and drove out of town, landing at the little beach in Huron. She spent the entire afternoon sitting on the rocks, taking in the gentle sound of water lapping at the shore. She willed the breeze to blow away every roiling thought, even as it dried every errant tear.

29

For a long time after Corinne left the office, Marcus just sat. Not working. Just sitting.

He was numb. Never in a million years would he have guessed the conversation of the day would go in that direction. It wasn't what he'd planned. It just happened.

Marcus shook his head every few seconds as the shock of it hit him over and over again. If he thought he'd messed up that Sunday after Cedar Point, it was nothing compared to this. His whole world had just exploded, and he'd caused it. Just him. Nobody else.

He couldn't even recognize himself in the man who'd been in the meeting with Corinne. *Who was that?*

Every bad thing that had ever happened in his life before today was nothing compared to this. The one person in the world that he thought he might care about the most, and he'd hurt her. The look on her face had been unmistakable. She had never even suspected.

Why the hell had he gone there? Never in his right frame of mind would he have chosen to reveal that information to her in that way. Never. Of course, he hadn't been in his right frame of mind lately. The thought filled him with frustration and an indefinable rage.

Marcus looked down at his desk. He gathered the papers and shoved them into the client folder. Then he got up and walked out.

Two hours and a hundred aimless miles later, the rage began to subside and numbness set in. These past two months since Corinne had shown up in Sutton had been a roller coaster ride like no other. But now, he was certain that ride was grounded.

Marcus returned to Sutton and pulled into his driveway. Once inside he dumped his wallet and keys on the hall table and headed for the kitchen. Pulling open the refrigerator door, he peered inside. Nothing looked good to eat, so instead he grabbed the lone beer that remained, a remnant from his former life.

He carried it out to the back deck, set it on the patio table, and sprawled on the outdoor sofa, arms folded across his chest, staring at nothing. The sounds of life occurring all around were lost on him: neighbors coming and going, children shouting as they played on swing sets, birds singing the afternoon away.

For all his plans to find out once and for all where he stood with Corinne, Marcus had instead thrown his very worst at her, all wrapped up in a dark and jaded attitude that he'd never met in himself before. Even he'd been stunned by it. Any person in their right mind would have been.

Except for Corinne. She didn't get angry or yell or walk out. Nothing normal like that. No, she talked about God.

Marcus closed his eyes and groaned. If God wanted to be part of his life so badly, fine. But why did it have to be so damn difficult? Couldn't He just say, "Hey," and let him get on with his life?

Marcus reached for the beer and saw that tiny beads of condensation had formed. He drew his finger down the side of the bottle and stared at the clear swath of glass. Then he drew a crossbar about a third of the way from the top.

Apparently not.

All Marcus had ever wanted was someone in his life to love, and to be loved by in return. He'd always thought that was a woman.

Well, he still did think that. But he had to admit there was some truth to what Corinne had said. He did have a hole in his heart. He'd just never thought it had anything to do with God.

Was it possible she was right about that? And if she was, what was he supposed to do about it?

22

If Corinne had thought that agreeing to be obedient to God's call on her life in Sutton meant that He'd make it easy for her, she now knew better. And it had become obvious that in spite of her earnest prayers since talking with Evelyn, deep down she was still fantasizing about happily ever after.

And so, in between the tears that she couldn't seem to keep from falling, Corinne spent the next week praying even more earnestly—both for Marcus and his salvation, and for her own ability to stay focused on God and obedient to Him through it all, whatever it all was.

Thus, it was a subdued Corinne who sat in the pew early that next Sunday morning, praying. Daniel and Becky arrived next. Having them there felt normal. They asked no questions and offered no advice, for which she was grateful. Of course, Corinne wasn't sure if they even knew all that had transpired since Cedar Point. She wasn't about to tell them.

In the last moments before the music began, Marcus slipped into the pew beside Daniel. Relieved to see him there once again, Corinne offered up a prayer of gratitude that he hadn't stayed away. She wanted to catch his eye and let him know that with a look, but he wouldn't meet her eye. It made her sad.

There was nothing she could do about it at present, though, so she turned her attention to the worship service.

As the pastor ended his sermon, her phone vibrated. She reached into her pocket to stop the buzz.

It vibrated again as they were singing the final hymn. Corinne grabbed it and saw that the caller was her sister. She silenced the phone again, planning to return the call as soon as the service was over.

She didn't get the chance. It buzzed for the third time before she could exit the noisy sanctuary, and a now worried Corinne plugged her other ear as she answered.

"Casey?" she said.

"Cori, thank God!"

"What's going on?" She stopped where she was, causing the foot traffic to swirl in another direction. Daniel, Becky, and Marcus gathered around her.

"Mom and Dad were in a car accident on the way to church this morning."

The room began to spin. "Oh, my God. Are they—?"

"They're alive. Injured, but I don't know how badly." Casey's voice broke. "I haven't gotten to see them yet." She burst into tears and could say no more.

Corinne couldn't breathe. She closed her eyes, and her knees buckled from beneath her. Strong arms encircled her and guided her to a nearby pew that was set against the back wall of the sanctuary.

She clutched the phone to her face, oblivious that all three of her companions were right by her side.

Casey spoke again. "Corinne, please come home. We need you here."

"Of course. I'll be there as soon as I can."

"Just be careful, okay?"

"I will. And Casey," she said, her voice choked with emotion, "tell them I love them."

"You're going to tell them yourself when you get here!" Casey said. "They're going to be okay. They have to be okay."

The next few minutes were a blur to Corinne. Someone hung up her phone. Someone handed her a tissue. Somehow, she told them what had happened.

Later she would recall Becky's fierce hug, and that Daniel prayed for her family. She would recall the quiet anguish on Marcus's face and the silent strength of his presence.

After that few minutes of initial terror and shock, Corinne's head began to clear. She took a deep breath and exhaled, knowing that she had to get on the road to be with her family. Thanking her friends for their love and concern, she hugged them all, then ran out of the church.

9

Just like that, Corinne was gone.

Marcus wondered if he'd ever see her again, because what reason would she have to come back?

It was a subdued trio who shared lunch at Daniel and Becky's house that afternoon. "Becky," Marcus said. "You'll keep in touch with Corinne, right?"

"Absolutely."

"I'd like to know, you know, how things are going."

"Of course." Becky thought for a moment. "But you can call her, too. I'm sure she'd appreciate all the support she can get."

Marcus hesitated. That wasn't gonna happen. He'd made things worse than ever, and he doubted that reaching out would seem like support to Corinne. But how could he tell his friends that? What he ended up saying was, "Things might be crazy for them. I wouldn't want to overwhelm her with calls on top of everything else."

Daniel studied his friend, lips pursed. "Marc, let's get a beer and go sit on the deck. What do you say?"

"Yeah, that's fine." Marcus got up to clear his plate from the table. Becky shooed him away and then turned to the sink. Daniel grabbed two beers from the fridge and led the way out the door.

He handed one to Marcus before settling into a deck chair and twisting the top off his bottle. After his first swig he said, "Good stuff on a hot day."

Marcus said nothing but sat down, the beer unopened and forgotten in his hand. Daniel scrutinized him again and then set his brew on the table. "All right, spill it. What happened?"

Marcus looked up. He stared at his friend and then said, "I told her about my past."

Daniel tipped his head back, whistling as he did so. "I take it that didn't go well."

Marcus shook his head. "I don't know."

"What do you mean?"

Marcus set his unopened bottle down and stared off into the trees. "I hadn't planned to bring it up, but it just came out." Then he shared the story of his business meeting with Corinne, including her response to his revelation. "I haven't talked to her all week since, which isn't unusual, contrary to what you might think." He looked up to read Daniel's expression and then continued. "But I figured today was the day to have it out, once and for all. To find out if there was any chance—" He stopped talking, and then grabbed the beer bottle, twisting the top off and taking a long pull. "And now she's gone."

"She'll be back."

"Will she? Do we know that for sure?"

Daniel tilted his head. "What are you saying?"

"This is the woman who picks up and moves every year. She says it's just because she wants to, but we don't know if that's true."

Daniel inhaled. "We have to take her at her word. There's no reason not to."

Marcus waved a hand. "Out at Cedar Point I asked if there'd ever been anyone who made her want to stay at any of the places she's lived."

"What'd she say?"

Marcus locked eyes on Daniel. "Nothing. She just shook her head. She wouldn't answer."

"That could mean anything."

Marcus's eyes were piercing as he replied, "That's right. It could mean *anything*."

Daniel grabbed his beer and sipped as he stared off into the sky, his countenance thoughtful. Marcus just sat. He had no thoughts. His mind was numb, as it had been ever since Corinne ran out of the church. As it had been ever since their meeting, actually. He rubbed a hand across his face and brushed his fingers back through his hair.

Daniel said, "Corinne seems to be a woman of deep faith."

"Yeah, I know." He leaned forward and rested his elbows on his knees. "Isn't there, like, some rule against divorce, you know, in your religion?"

"It's not the preferred way of doing things. But it's not an automatic out, either."

Marcus narrowed his eyes. "What does that even mean?"

Daniel took a deep breath and let it out. "Well, when God created humanity, His perfect plan included marriage between one man and one woman, for life."

"Pfft. Guess that plan failed."

"Not really."

Marcus looked incredulous. "Uh, I make my living on the failure of that plan."

"No, you make your living on the choices people make."

Marcus was silent as he contemplated that perspective.

"See, God's plan included perfection in every aspect of life, relationships and everything else. But He also, in His wisdom, gave humankind a choice."

Marcus wagged his finger at Daniel. "That does not seem very wise to me. He had to know people would want to go their own way."

"He did know."

Marcus stuttered in surprise and Daniel continued. "God wants to be in relationship with us, and yes, He could force us to be. But He wants us to *want* to be in relationship with Him. And so, He gives us the choice."

Now Marcus was listening intently.

"The original people made the same choice that you and I and everyone else on this planet make every day of our lives. We go our own ways. And because we do, we are separated from God." Daniel stopped and collected his thoughts for a moment. "But that doesn't stop God from wanting a relationship with us, and it doesn't stop us from needing a relationship with Him."

Marcus thought of Corinne's explanation about the hole in his heart. He'd been skeptical of the idea that God was the only Being who could fill it. He didn't want to believe it, but here was his friend saying essentially the same thing. Could it be true? "So, what, then?" He asked. "We get in a relationship with God by going to church and listening to a sermon?" He huffed and shook his head. "If that's it, it's not working for me, buddy."

"That's not it."

Marcus was confused. "That's what you guys do."

"Yes, but we do those things as a result of our relationship with God. Those things aren't the relationship itself."

Marcus closed his eyes and rubbed his fingers across his forehead. "You're going to have to explain."

Daniel sat forward in his seat. "God still has His plan of perfection. But that plan is implemented in eternity, not in our physical lives here on this earth." He tapped the arm of his chair. "This earth, and everything in it, is tainted by our choice to 'go our own way'. But this life is also where we choose whether we want to be in relationship with God for all eternity, or not. If we do want that, God has provided a way for it to happen. He will walk with us here in this imperfect physical life so we can walk with Him in that perfect eternal one."

Marcus took this in. "Okay."

"Because God is perfect and holy, He cannot abide in the presence of sin, which is what our choice to reject Him is. So, He provided a sacrifice to cover that sin for us. We could never do it ourselves, because we are continually sinful. That sacrifice had to be made by someone who was without sin, and the only being who fits that bill is God Himself."

"What are you saying, God sacrificed Himself?"

"Sort of. He sent His Son to earth to live among humans, as a human—but a sinless one, because He is also God Himself. And that Son, Jesus Christ, was crucified on the cross to pay the penalty for our sinfulness, so that when we accept His sacrificial gift, we can be forgiven and return to the presence of God."

Marcus stared at his friend as he thought. He'd never heard this before. On the one hand, it sounded like craziness. But on the other...

"So, this Jesus died on a cross to pay for our sins?" he asked.

"That's right."

"Then what's the point? If it's going to pay for all the sins, or whatever, and everybody goes back to being in relationship with God, why bother with the whole unpleasant business?"

"It doesn't pay for all the sins. Don't forget the choice part. Everybody gets to choose whether they accept that gift or not. God wants us to and offers it to us—and sometimes strongly encourages us to take it." He stopped to let that sink in. "But we still get to make the choice. Those that decide against it, are *not* in relationship with God."

"Ever?"

Daniel shook his head. "Ever."

"What happens to them?"

"They're separated from God forever, eternally."

Marcus lifted his chin as the pieces clicked into place. "You mean hell."

"That's right. Heaven is with God. Hell is without Him."

The two men fell silent. Marcus's brain was firing again, and he knew there was a whole lot to think about in what his friend had just shared. But for right now, he still had one very important question.

"You said that divorce wasn't an automatic out. What did you mean?"

"Divorce fits in with all the other choices we make that go against God's perfect plan. It also fits in with all the other choices that are covered by Jesus' death on the cross when we accept that gift of salvation."

Marcus scrutinized Daniel's face. "You're saying it can be forgiven."

"Yes."

"Okay, but it doesn't undo it."

"No, it doesn't," Daniel said. "We can be forgiven but there are always consequences for the choices we've made. Baggage. We both know life is full of that."

"Yeah." Marcus thought this over. "Such as, God is willing to forgive me, but Corinne might not be."

Daniel hesitated. "It's a possibility. But more than that, even if she does, the consequences from those relationships affect all the rest of your life, one way or another."

Marcus chewed on the corner of his lip. "And if people followed that perfect plan of marriage between one man and one woman for life, there'd be way less baggage."

"Yeah, that's right. It doesn't make everything perfect, though, because—"

"Imperfect world," Marcus cut in.

"Yep." Daniel continued. "But the commitment to remain in that relationship encourages two people to work through issues together and to walk through life side by side as teammates, rather than as adversaries."

Marcus dropped his head. There was nothing he had ever wanted more, but he had never been able to accomplish it. "Like you and Becky," he said.

Daniel drew in a deep breath before responding. "We try to work through the tough times as partners instead of as enemies. It's not always easy, but it's always worth it."

They were both quiet again, for a long time. When Marcus spoke up, it was to say, "I've got a lot to think about."

"Anytime you wanna talk."

"Thanks, man."

2

Marcus walked in the door of Maddie's the next morning and said, "I've got questions."

Roger shook his hand and said, "Okay, let's get to them."

In between ordering and receiving and eating food, Marcus shared the events of his week: Tuesday's meeting, the call Corinne received at church, and his conversation with Daniel. Roger stayed quiet, taking in every word.

He shook his head when Marcus finished. "That's a heavy week."

"Yeah."

Roger looked at his watch. "Do you have meetings lined up this morning?"

"Uh," Marcus pulled out his phone and looked at his calendar. "No, I do not."

"Good. Let me make a couple of calls and then if you're okay with it, let's take the morning off and work through this."

Marcus was relieved. "That sounds good." He called Irene and told her he'd be in after lunch. "I appreciate this, Roger."

"Of course. There is nothing in this world as important as the conversation we're having right now, Marcus."

The two men drove separately to Roger's house. Nancy met them at the door and ushered them out to the back patio, which was set with two chairs, iced tea, and a plate of cookies.

"One of your calls must have been to your wife," Marcus said.

"It was," Roger replied. "I also told her that we'd just had breakfast, but it did no good." He winked at Nancy, and she blew him a kiss before disappearing into the house.

Marcus and Roger settled themselves in the shade of the large pin oak. "What's your first question, Marcus?" Roger wanted to know.

Marcus took a deep breath. "Everything Daniel told me yesterday, it all fits with the stuff I've been hearing lately—from you, from Corinne, in the sermons at church. But what I want to know is, where's it coming from? How do you guys know this stuff?"

"That's a great question. And the answer is, the Bible."

Marcus arched a brow. "Really."

"Yes, indeed. The Bible is the revealed Word of God. You could say it's our handbook for getting to know Him and the perfect plan He has for His creation."

Marcus was skeptical. "Can you show me?"

Roger picked up a book from the table, which Marcus had not even noticed until that moment. It was a black, leather-bound volume, and had, as he saw when Roger opened it, lots of pencil markings and notes.

For the next hour, Roger turned to passage after passage, reading the text to Marcus and showing him where in God's Word to find the answers to the questions he was asking: God's perfect creation, His relationship with humankind, man's disastrous choice, the blueprint for marriage, all in Genesis. Humanity's inability to fulfill God's law and be holy, all throughout the Old Testament. The revelation of God's plan to save mankind, sprinkled among the prophets. The fulfillment of those prophecies in the birth, death, and resurrection of Jesus Christ in Luke and the other gospels.

"And there's so much more," Roger said, caressing the cover of the holy book. "Beginning to end, every word in here is for the purpose of making God known to us. We can never exhaust the riches of what He has to teach us through His Word."

Marcus ran his fingers through his hair and then pointed at the book as it rested in Roger's lap. "You've been studying that book a long time, haven't you?"

"Ever since God called me to Him."

"Which started the Sunday you drove a young lady named Nancy to church."

"Yes, that's right. You know, to this day I don't know how it all came about, but the pastor paid me a visit that week, after my very first time in church, and before I knew it he had me going to a men's Bible study and was checking in on my progress on the reading plan he'd outlined for me." He shook his head in wonder. "I've been studying this book ever since."

Roger opened his mouth to speak again, hesitated, and then plunged forward. "It was a few months before I came to know Christ as my Savior. I knew nothing about God when I started, and I had lots of questions."

"Like me."

"Yes. Some of the verses that got me there were from Romans, which is one of the first books the pastor had me read."

"You didn't start at the beginning? In that Genesis book?"

"Not at first. You see, in very broad strokes, the first part of the Bible gives us the history—the why—behind our need. The second part tells us how God meets that need." He opened the Bible to Romans 3:10 and read, "There is no one righteous, not even one." He skipped down to verse 23 and read, "For all have sinned and fall short of the glory of God." Then he turned the page to chapter 5, verse 12, and read, "Therefore, just as sin entered the world through one man, and death through sin, in this way death spread to all men, because all sinned." And in 6:23, "For the wages of sin is death, but the gift of God is eternal life in Christ Jesus our Lord."

Roger looked up. "So, there we've got the bad news—the very bad news—that we're all doomed, but we also have the first indication of hope." He turned back a page to chapter 5, verses 8 and 9. "But God demonstrates His own love for us in that while we were still sinners, Christ died for us! Much more then, since we have now been declared righteous by His blood, we will be saved through Him from wrath."

He shook his head. "It's an amazing thing to think that God offers this gift to us while we're eyeballs deep in our own sinfulness. He's willing to do that for us; that's how much He loves us." He smiled in amazement and then continued.

"So now we have the price paid. Now we have to confess and accept and turn to Him, and here's how." Roger thumbed the pages until he reached Romans 10:9-10. "If you confess with your mouth, 'Jesus is Lord,' and believe in your heart that God raised Him from the dead, you will be saved." He finished with verse 13 in the same chapter.

"For everyone who calls on the name of the Lord will be saved."

By the conclusion of this recitation of verses, Marcus was trembling from head to foot. Roger closed the Bible and laid it on the table. He reached over and placed his hand on Marcus's shoulder. "Son, God has been calling you. He wants you. Will you come to Him?"

Marcus's breath came out in a rush and as he gasped for air, he nodded his head. "Yes," he said. "Yes, I want this. Will you help me?"

And right there on the back patio, under the pin oak tree, Roger led Marcus in prayer to confess his sin and accept Jesus as his Savior.

3

"Amen."

"Thank you, Lord Jesus," Roger breathed.

Marcus swiped the tears from his eyes before he raised his head. Roger was grinning from ear to ear and his own eyes were bright. He stood and pulled Marcus to his feet, wrapping him in a huge bear hug as he did so. "Welcome to the family, brother," he whispered.

Something like a sob escaped Marcus's lips, and the tears started to flow once again. After a few moments they pulled apart and just stared at one another until, without warning, a bubble of laughter escaped Marcus's lips. "Oh, man," he exclaimed. He was laughing and crying at the same time.

Roger clapped him on the shoulder, then they both collapsed back down on their chairs.

Marcus sniffled and then pinched his nose to try to keep it from running. Roger offered him a clean handkerchief, and Marcus used it to mop up his face. After that Roger picked up the two glasses of tea and handed him one. Marcus took a sip and then chugged half the contents. Then he leaned back in his chair and sighed.

In another moment, however, he turned thoughtful. "Now what?" he asked.

"I think cookies are next for the moment." He picked up the plate and offered it to Marcus, who selected a handful. "Celebration cookies," Roger explained.

"Yeah." Marcus took a bite and then downed them all in short order. Cookies had never tasted so good.

"Then," Roger continued. "I think it's time to get you on a reading plan to know God better."

Marcus agreed. "I need a Bible."

"Why don't we drive down to the bookstore right now? They've got a nice men's study Bible that would be perfect to get you started."

After the bookstore, Marcus returned and had lunch with Roger and Nancy. It was good, and he didn't just mean the food. Nancy was as excited as her husband was over Marcus's decision and couldn't stop beaming at him the entire meal.

All that week, Marcus holed up at home in the evenings and devoured the reading plan Roger had laid out for him. Everything was so new and such a different way of understanding the world. Roger had warned him that he'd come away with more questions than answers, especially at first, but it didn't matter. He was soaking it up.

He was blown away by how little he had understood life. As he looked back, even just to a week ago, it seemed as if he'd been living under a cold, wet blanket that he hadn't even known was there. Now that weight was lifted, and he could see light for the first time ever.

He couldn't wait to tell Daniel. He wanted to tell Corinne too, but he had no idea how to do that, or if she'd even want to hear from him. He pushed the thought aside, uncertain what to do with it.

He arrived at Maddie's a bit early for lunch on Friday and settled himself in their regular booth. Truth be told, he was nervous about how to share this news. What words were there to convey what he had experienced?

Maddie caught his eye and tipped her head. Marcus lifted his hand in greeting. She came over and asked, "You want something to drink while you're waiting?"

"Iced tea would be great; thank you! Would you go ahead and bring one for Daniel, too?"

Maddie wrote it on her pad and left to fill the order. Suddenly Marcus wondered what her story was and realized he'd never even thought to wonder that before. When she returned and set the glasses on the table, Marcus said, "So how are you doing, Maddie?"

Maddie stopped in her tracks. "I'm doing fine." She stared at Marcus. "How are you doing?"

"I'm doing all right. Thanks for asking." Marcus ducked his head, a little embarrassed.

After one more sideways look Maddie moved on to the next table.

At ten minutes after Daniel blew in the door and slid into the booth. "Sorry I'm late," he said. "Got caught by the homeowner at the last minute."

"No problem."

"What a week." Daniel leaned back in his seat and blew out his breath.

"Busy?"

"Crazy," Daniel said. "Change orders, back orders, screwed up orders...what a mess." He lifted the glass of iced tea to his lips and downed it. "That hits the spot. Thanks."

"Sure." Marcus leaned forward and tapped the tabletop. "I'm telling you, though, you need to hire someone to take on part of that workload."

"Yeah, yeah, yeah." Daniel brushed him off. "I don't even have time to think about it." He looked around the room for Maddie and caught her eye. She made her way over and the two men placed their orders.

"Well, invest some time in the off-season, and then you'll be ready for next year."

"I suppose." Daniel looked thoughtful. "Honestly, I don't have the first idea how to go about that."

"Maybe that's where you need to start then—by finding the people who can help you 'go about that'."

Daniel raised his eyebrows. "Listen to you! All professional and full of advice."

"Nothing I haven't been telling you forever." His eyes twinkled as he took a sip of his tea.

"I know something about that," Daniel said pointedly.

"Speaking of that," Marcus began, and then cleared his throat. "I had a lot of questions after our conversation Sunday afternoon."

Daniel stopped short and stared at him. "Uh-huh."

"I've been meeting Roger Beck for breakfast on Monday mornings. Wasn't sure if you knew that."

"Go on."

"This past Monday he walked me through passages in the Bible that answered my questions and made me realize what's been missing in my life." He took a shaky breath and continued. "Then he helped me pray to accept Jesus as my Savior."

Daniel stared at him, his mouth hanging open. "Dude!" he yelled, slapping his hands against the back of his head. "That is the best news ever!"

Marcus needn't have worried about how to tell his friend his news. He just said the words. And Daniel's response couldn't have been more perfect. Marcus was touched. Grateful. It felt good that it meant so much to him. But he could think of nothing more to say. He just sat there with a huge grin on his face.

Maddie threaded her way through the tables and deposited two lunch plates in front of them. "Maddie!" Daniel exclaimed. "Guess what? We have a new brother in Christ! Marcus became a Christian this week."

Marcus was stunned by Daniel's proclamation; he hadn't quite expected him to shout it from the rooftops. Then he stopped short. *Hold on, we? Was Maddie a Christian, too?*

Maddie gave him an appraising look, but the corners of her mouth were tugging upward, desperate to break free. "Did he, now? Will wonders never cease!" Then she winked and turned back toward the kitchen.

Marcus snorted; he couldn't help it. He'd never paid attention to it before, but Maddie could be funny. In a crusty, understated sort of a way.

Then the two men shared their first prayer together as brothers in Christ and proceeded to polish off their celebratory lunch. Marcus was amazed, again, at how different life felt. It was crazy; nothing had changed, and yet everything had.

He was even more amazed when they went to pay their bill, and Maddie told them it was on the house.

4

When Becky saw Marcus in the parking lot before church Sunday morning, she rushed over and wrapped him in a fierce, Becky-sized bear hug. When she pulled away, her eyes were glistening, and she was beaming. "Welcome to the family," she squeaked, then tittered at herself and pulled a tissue from her purse to blow her nose.

Marcus was touched. "Thanks, Bec." Daniel joined them as they walked toward the church. Marcus recovered a bit and looked sideways at Becky. "So does this make you my sister?"

Becky's eyes widened in delight. "You bet it does!"

Once inside Daniel said, "Let's go share your good news with Pastor Stephen."

Pastor Stephen's kind face registered his delight at the news. He grabbed Marcus by the hand and drew him into a one-armed embrace. "Praise be to God! We've been praying for you every week."

Marcus was startled by this news. Who had been praying for him? And how did they come to do that? He was so taken up with these musings he almost didn't notice that with every person they said good morning to, Daniel was sharing the news.

It wasn't until they met up with Roger that it all became clear. The men's weekly prayer group that both Roger and the pastor were part of. That's who had been praying.

After the service there were more handshakes and hugs and welcomes from the congregation as the word spread. One of the men invited him to the prayer group. Another invited him to a Bible study. These people were joy-filled to see him come to faith.

Marcus was undone. He had never experienced such belonging—not in his family, not at school, not even in marriage. It was incredible.

Daniel and Becky insisted that he join them for Sunday lunch again. He didn't mind, although his thoughts and his emotions were in a complete uproar. All he could do was shake his head every few minutes. Daniel and Becky exchanged winks with each other and let him be.

Afterward they drifted out to enjoy the sun on the back deck. As they soaked up the rays, Marcus began to relax. He thought back over the week—and realized he hadn't been obsessing over Corinne. In fact, he realized he hadn't thought about her and her family very much at all. He felt guilty about that and asked, "Hey, Becky, have you heard from Corinne?"

"I have."

"How are her folks? Are they okay?"

"A bunch of broken bones, but nothing life threatening, thank the Lord. Mobility is going to be an issue while they heal, so it sounds like Corinne is going to be there for a while, helping out."

"Wow," he mused. "That's going to be a lot."

"Yes, and her sister's baby is due anytime. So, they've got their hands full." Becky looked over at Marcus. "I take it you didn't try to call."

Marcus shook his head. "I didn't. I—"

"Hey, it's all right," Daniel chimed in. "You've had a lot going on this week."

"Most important week of your entire life," Becky added.

Marcus looked from one to the other of them. They both nodded. "I guess it was, wasn't it?"

"Absolutely!" Becky said. "And I know Corinne will understand. She'll be as happy for you as we are. You should call her this week and tell her."

Marcus smiled wryly at Becky. "I think I'll wait to tell her in person."

Becky opened her mouth to argue, but Daniel raised a hand to quiet her. She stopped and regarded Marcus. "Okay. I won't say anything."

"Thank you, Becky," Marcus said. "I appreciate that."

Marcus did want to reach out to Corinne. The truth is he was still afraid to, even with his good news to share. What if she rejected him? It was easier to be the one who did the walking away. That's what he'd always done whenever the conflict started in whatever relationship he was in.

The thing was, though, the only reason there was any conflict between him and Corinne was because of his own behavior. Corinne wasn't nagging him to be someone different. She wasn't haranguing him to provide some kind of lifestyle he was incapable of. Those things had always been easy to walk away from.

But all of that was from his old life. It wasn't even happening now. Plus, everything he'd been learning from Daniel and from Roger was that his decision to accept Christ changed everything—even his human relationships. The problem was, he was at a complete loss as to what that should look like.

Every so often he picked up his phone and started a text message to Corinne, only to delete it before sending. He simply had no idea what to say.

The next Sunday it was just Marcus and Daniel in church. Becky was absent.

"Where's your wife?" Marcus wanted to know.

"Indianapolis."

Marcus started in surprise. "Are you serious? What's she doing?"

"She's helping Corinne and her sister. She wanted to do something, and with school starting up in a couple of weeks, it was now or never."

Marcus thought this over. "I wish there was something I could do to help."

"I know what you mean," Daniel replied. "The good thing is that, as Christians, there's one thing we can always do, no matter what."

"What's that?" Marcus asked.

"Pray."

That stopped Marcus up short. Pray? He hadn't thought about that. Prayer for him had been limited to mealtime and church, and those only in the past couple of months. Since his conversion, he had thanked God over and over again for saving him, but so far that was it. It was obvious he had a lot to learn about being a Christian.

"Tell you what," Daniel said. "After church let's get some lunch, and when we pray for our meal, we can include Corinne and all of her family. Sound good?"

"Sounds perfect!"

The two men grabbed burgers and fries at a fast-food joint after church. Maddie's was closed on Sundays; now Marcus understood why.

As they dove into the meal after praying, he had a question. "So, do you pray for people a lot?"

Daniel unwrapped his sandwich. "Yeah. I've prayed for you for years."

Marcus was stunned. "You have?"

"Mm hmm." Daniel took a bite of his hamburger and watched his friend.

Marcus nibbled on a fry. "How come it took so long, you know, to get answered?"

"You're stubborn," he replied and smirked at his friend.

Marcus guffawed. He took a bite of his own sandwich and as he chewed, thought that over. "Yeah, I suppose I am."

They ate in silence for a bit, Marcus deep in thought. "But He always answers, right?"

Daniel bobbed his head from side to side. "He always answers, but it's not always the answer we're hoping for."

"Why not? I mean, you were praying for what He wanted, right?"

"I was," Daniel agreed, "but remember that freedom to choose I told you about?" Marcus nodded. "God gave you the option to either accept or decline His invitation."

That thought sobered Marcus. How easy it might have been never to have answered the call. He shuddered at the thought.

"I gotta tell you though," Daniel said, "how glad I am that you finally accepted."

"Thank you for never giving up on me. I mean that."

"Absolutely." Daniel wadded up the paper from his burger and tossed it on the table. "You know what else I haven't given up on?"

"What's that?"

"That you might beat me at 21 someday."

"Oh hell, I beat you all the time!" Marcus stopped short, and then deflated. "There's probably a rule against cussing in God's perfect plan, isn't there?"

"It's not the preferred way." Daniel's eyes twinkled as he spoke, but then he turned serious. "Just remember, it's a lifelong journey, and you're just getting started."

"Ain't that the truth." Marcus shook his head but then stared at his friend. "I do owe you a butt kicking, though, for that little stunt you pulled last time we played." He leaned forward and whispered. "Does that work?"

"Good enough," Daniel said. "Let's go."

5

That night while Marcus was sitting in his living room with his feet propped up and his Bible on his lap, he attempted his first solo prayer for Corinne. At first, he tried to incorporate the language he recalled from Pastor Stephen's prayers in church. That didn't feel right at all. Next, he tried repeating the words Daniel used at lunch, but even that felt foreign. None of them were his words.

Scowling, he lowered his feet to the floor, leaned forward in his seat, and bowed his head over his folded hands. He sat there, silent and contemplative. If he were asking another person to do something for someone he cared about, what would he say?

Unfortunately, that rumination didn't help either, and so he just started talking. "I feel like I have so much catching up to do, so much to learn. I wish I had taken Daniel up on his invitation a long time ago. But I'm here now, and I'm glad You didn't give up on me."

The tension seeped out of his shoulders, and Marcus felt a sense of peace. "Thank you," he said, in awe because of it. For a few moments he just sat and soaked it in. When he continued, he said, "I want to pray for Corinne. For her family too. I wish I could help them, but I don't know if Corinne would want to hear from me and I don't want to upset her. She's got a lot going on right now."

Marcus thought for a moment. "Daniel says we can always pray, no matter what, so even if I can't help in some physical way, I want to do that. Please take care of her and her whole family." He stopped. The statement felt so ineffective, almost like a copout. "I don't know how to do this, God."

But he didn't move. He kept the posture of prayer, even though he didn't know what words to say. He thought back to Roger's prayers. They always sounded like he was talking to a respected friend about whatever was on his mind.

"Corinne and her folks, they're part of Your family, right? So that means You love them and care for them. Please bring them peace even in the midst of what they're going through, like You did for me a few minutes ago."

Marcus leaned back and rested his head against the recliner. Crazy as it sounded, he had known without a doubt that it was God who brought that peacefulness to him. God was making Himself known, just like everyone around him had been saying for months.

After a few minutes he leaned forward again and rested his head in his hands. "You know God, I do want to talk to Corinne. I want to do things differently, as a Christian this time, instead of as who I was before. But where do I start? Do I tell her about accepting Jesus first or do I apologize for what happened? It just doesn't seem like the right time to do either of those things."

His chest squeezed as he thought about his past and how he had revealed it to Corinne. "I wouldn't be surprised if she didn't believe it, given that stunt I pulled in my office that day, but I care about her, God. I know it's weird, because we don't know each other very well. I don't understand it, but I just know that I do. The thing is, with my history—" he exhaled. "She doesn't deserve that, You know?"

The ache in his chest was palpable, and Marcus remained as he was for a long time. His prayer now was a silent plea from the heart, too deep to be expressed in words. This prayer was lifted by the Spirit to the throne of God even though Marcus knew nothing about such things.

When he did stir, it was to speak these last few words, "I hope that was okay as a prayer, God. Amen."

6

Becky was back in church next Sunday, and she and Daniel invited Marcus to join them for lunch afterward so she could catch him up on the situation in Indianapolis.

"They've got home health services coming in daily to help, which is good. Corinne's sister is nearly full term and can't do any heavy lifting."

"How's Corinne doing with all that?" Marcus wanted to know.

"She dived right into learning whatever she had to in order to take care of her parents." Becky smiled as she thought of her friend. "She's a hard worker. Not getting a lot of sleep, though, between her parents and trying to keep up with her business."

"That has to be tough," Daniel said.

"So, were you helping with her parents' care, too?" Marcus asked.

"No, I did some cooking and cleaning and helped with the kids." She paused. "Casey has two..." Her voice trailed off and she looked down at her plate.

"That makes sense," Marcus agreed. "You love kids, right?"

"Yeah," she whispered. "I do."

"How come you guys don't have any?" Marcus blurted out.

Becky froze, and then looked up at Daniel with haunted eyes.

"Dude!" Daniel said and shot out of his chair. He was at Becky's side in a heartbeat. He wrapped his arms around her and held her close.

"What?" Marcus asked, looking at each of them. "What'd I say?"

Daniel widened his eyes and shook his head. In that split second, the truth crashed down upon Marcus. His friends didn't have kids—but not because they didn't want to.

"Oh," he said. "I didn't know." He felt stupid. *How could I not have known?*

Neither of them answered. Becky was sobbing and Daniel was comforting her. Marcus felt very much in the way—and very much alone. Daniel was his best friend, but that would never trump the marriage relationship. Daniel and Becky would always come before Daniel and Marcus. As they should. He didn't begrudge them their closeness; he just wished he could figure that out for his own life.

Then he chided himself. Why had his thoughts gone in that direction? It was selfish, considering the moment. But then, Marcus had always been pretty self-centered where his friends were concerned. Why would he expect anything different from himself now? *Because of God,* he thought. Then he silently prayed, *God help me to be different.*

Eventually Becky's sobs subsided, and she used a tissue to dry her eyes.

Marcus looked up. "I'm sorry," he said to her. "I didn't mean to hurt you."

Becky sniffled. "I know you didn't."

Daniel said nothing. He was still focused on Becky.

Marcus pushed back from the table and stood. "I'm going to go." He turned and walked out of the kitchen.

A moment later, a chair scraped, and Becky ran after him. "Wait, Marcus," she said, touching him on the arm. "Please don't leave."

"I feel like I'm intruding."

"You know better than that!" Becky said.

Marcus looked up at Daniel, who was leaning against the doorway to the kitchen. He looked like he agreed with Marcus on this one. "I'm sorry," he said to Daniel. When Daniel didn't respond, Marcus gave Becky a small, sad smile and walked out the door.

It was a long Sunday afternoon and an even longer sleepless night. Marcus has never been at odds with his friend before. Daniel was always so easy-going that Marcus had never seen him shaken. As he contemplated the events of the day, he realized that Daniel never talked about personal issues. They discussed business and the ups and downs of Marcus's life, but never Daniel's. He pondered this at length, wondering if it was Daniel's choice or because of his own self-centeredness. He was pretty sure he knew the answer to that question.

Roger's advice, when they met the next morning, was prayer. Not just for the conflict, but for his friends' sorrow. "Praying for others helps us to experience empathy, Marcus, and it brings them comfort and guidance."

"Do I reach out?" Marcus wanted to know.

"Give him a little time," Roger said. "If you guys don't connect on Friday over lunch as you normally do, then reach out."

And so, Marcus added Daniel and Becky to his prayers. Still uncertain about what words to use, still regretting that he'd been stubborn about faith for so long, he was nonetheless grateful to know that he could come to God at any time and talk with Him about anything.

It's what he'd wanted all his life—and hadn't even realized it.

7

Friday found Marcus at Maddie's Diner early again but uncertain if Daniel would show. They hadn't talked all week, which in itself wasn't unusual. They almost always met for lunch on Fridays, but it was often without having seen each other throughout the week.

Marcus just wasn't sure how things were between them, that's all. Daniel hadn't said one word after, "Dude!" on Sunday. So, as he sat waiting, Marcus prayed. Not out loud, but inside his head.

When Daniel pulled open the glass door at the stroke of noon, Marcus's relief was palpable.

"Hey," Daniel said as he slid into the seat.

"Hi," Marcus responded.

There followed an uncomfortable and unusual silence between them. Marcus cast about in his mind for something to say but kept coming up short. His loss for words seemed to characterize him more and more these past few months. He had always prided himself on having an answer for everything.

Whether it was a good one or not was beside the point.

Now it was as if knowing the truth about God made him realize how very little he knew about anything else.

As he was lost in these thoughts, Daniel cleared his throat and said, "Hey, listen. I need to apologize."

"You—what?" Marcus was confused.

"I know you weren't trying to be hurtful. I'm just protective of Becky when it comes to that subject."

"I can understand that. But I don't understand what you're apologizing for."

Daniel looked away before answering. "Becky and I don't talk about this with anyone." He stopped and exhaled.

"Hey, it's your private business. You don't owe me any explanations."

Daniel placed his arms on the table and leaned toward Marcus. "Yes, I do. When you realized what was going on, you were sorry. That was evident. But I didn't want to forgive you."

Marcus recoiled. He'd been contemplating for quite some time what life was going to be like if Corinne didn't forgive him. Now he realized that the same thing could have happened with his best friend, too. The horribleness of having someone you care about reject you struck him square in the chest.

Daniel pushed on. "I was pissed at how things are, and you were a handy target." He shook his head. "That scared me."

Marcus took a deep breath and forced himself to concentrate. "I don't understand. What do you mean it scared you?"

"You know the Lord's Prayer, right? 'Forgive us our sins as we forgive those who sin against us.' If I can hold onto my anger that easily, especially misguided anger, what does it say about my relationship with God? Is it even real?"

"Of course it is!" Marcus said. "You're forgiven, not perfect. Isn't that what you've been telling me?"

Daniel blinked in surprise.

Marcus's brain was back to work. "When I prayed for Jesus to forgive my sins and be my Savior, I wasn't just praying for sins I'd committed in the past. Right?" he asked, checking his logic with Daniel. "There will be more in the future. Faith is a journey. I have to make sure I'm on the path and if I wander off, get back on. So do you!"

A slow and grateful smile formed on Daniel's face. "Well, listen to you."

Maddie arrived to take their order, and on the one hand Marcus was grateful for the respite. He'd never experienced an uncertain Daniel before.

When she left, however, he returned to it, knowing there was more that needed to be said. "What have you done to get back on the path, Daniel?"

"I've been praying," Daniel said. "Becky and I have talked—a lot." He opened his mouth to speak again, but then closed it and dropped his head. "That's what she and Corinne were praying about after the cookout. At first, I wasn't sure how I felt about it, the fact that Becky shared it with her, but then I realized she needs a friend to talk to sometimes." He looked up at Marcus. "Corinne seems to be a good one for that. Anyway, I knew I needed to come here today and ask for your forgiveness." Uncertainty crept into his eyes, and a little bit of discomfort. "So will you forgive me?"

"Absolutely, man," Marcus reached out a hand, which Daniel shook gratefully. "God knows you've put up with enough from me over the years." At this both men laughed, and the tension broke.

Then Marcus added, "You know, I've been praying this week too, for you guys, I mean."

Daniel sat back and stared at Marcus, his eyes unexpectedly bright. "Thank you," he said. "That means more to me than you could ever possibly know."

8

Three months ago, Marcus had just been a regular guy. He practiced law, played basketball, and socialized with friends. None of those things had changed, but he himself had. Now he saw the world through a different lens, and his old way of doing life was no longer satisfying.

"There's a lot of broken crap in my life, Roger!" he said one Monday morning over breakfast.

"I can relate to that. There was in mine, too," Roger said. "Still is sometimes."

Marcus scowled into his coffee. "I didn't think becoming a Christian would make me feel worse about myself."

"Just remember, Marcus, God has forgiven you for your sins."

Despite his recent wise counsel to his friend, Marcus still struggled to remember that truth for himself.

"I know," he agreed reluctantly.

"And He's at work in you."

Marcus quirked an eyebrow. "Are you sure?"

"Absolutely. You're aware that you've fallen short, and you want to be better. That's a good thing. Focus on Him rather than on your shortcomings, and He will guide you along the way."

Easy to say, harder to do, Marcus thought. He wanted to make things happen, but he was learning, slowly, that God worked in His own time and His own way. Accepting that truth left him with just his thoughts, and they were driving him crazy.

Daniel's solution was to put him to physical labor.

"I don't know anything about construction," he objected.

"That's the beauty of it," Daniel argued. "You don't have to."

"What's this thing called again?"

"Habitat for Humanity. Volunteers work alongside qualified families to help them build an affordable home. No experience required."

So, Marcus picked up a hammer and went to work with Daniel on Saturdays. He learned a little bit about construction and developed some blisters in the process. He also came to respect his friend's profession on a whole new level.

Pastor Stephen's solution was to surround him with other Christian men in study, prayer, and service, which he willingly agreed to, and where he also learned many new things.

And Marcus's solution? When his thoughts still threatened to overwhelm, he hit the basketball court. Nearly every day, as it turned out. All the additional exercise slimmed him down and toned him up. He rather enjoyed his new look.

Apparently, he wasn't the only one.

Marcus was hard at work on some contract paperwork one afternoon in mid-September when in walked Abigail Fredrickson. They had closed her case the week before, so there was no reason for her to be there.

"Hello, Marcus," she said, arranging herself in one of the chairs across from his desk.

"Ms. Jackson! I don't think we have an appointment." He flipped to his calendar to check.

"We don't." She leaned against the arm of the chair. "I just wanted to stop in and say thank you. Everything came out just right in the divorce."

"You're welcome," Marcus replied. "I'm glad it worked out." He stood up. "I need to get back to—"

"You were amazing."

Marcus moved toward the door, a sense of unease building. "Just doing my job."

"Listen," Abigail said, turning in her chair. "I thought maybe we could celebrate, over dinner." She raised her eyebrows at him.

Marcus shook his head. "I'm sorry. That's not possible."

Abigail got up and sauntered toward him. "But why not? I'm not a client anymore." She trailed a finger along the buttons of his shirt.

Marcus deflected her hand with his forearm. "The answer's no, and it's time for you to leave. Irene!" He called down the hall to his secretary.

There was the slam of a door and then hurried footsteps in the hall. Abigail looked Marcus up and down. "You can still change your mind."

Irene stopped in the doorway, surprised by the scene before her.

"Would you please see Ms. Jackson to the door?"

Abigail's eyes turned icy in an instant. Marcus was transported back in time to every breakup he'd ever experienced, and the pure hatred that so quickly replaced the heat of attraction.

"Yes, sir," Irene said. "This way, ma'am."

Abigail stalked past Marcus, rounded the corner, and stomped down the hallway.

Marcus stood frozen, holding his breath until he heard the slam of the front door. Then he gulped for air and stumbled back across the office to collapse against his desk. In a few moments, Irene peeked her head in the doorway and said, "Are you okay?"

"How in the hell did that happen?" he demanded.

"I was in the bathroom," Irene said.

"Oh, my God," Marcus exclaimed. He retreated behind his desk and collapsed in the chair, holding his head in his hands.

"I'm sorry!" Irene's voice was choked.

Marcus's head shot up. "No! Oh no, Irene, it's not your fault." He abandoned his chair and hustled over to her.

Irene's eyes were bright with barely contained tears. Marcus took her by the elbow and led her to an armchair. Then he grabbed a box of tissues off the side table and handed it to her. He sat in the opposite chair and watched her. Once she had collected herself, he gestured toward the front door of their office. "I got caught off guard by that is all. I'm sorry for yelling at you." He drew in a shaky breath. "Will you forgive me?"

She nodded, crumpling the tissue in her hand.

"Thank you." Marcus looked toward the ceiling. "Who'd have thought we should have to lock the door just to take a bathroom break?"

"I guess we could start."

"Might not be a bad idea." Marcus rubbed his hands across his face and then swiped at his shirt, as if to get the feel of that woman's hands off him. "Ugh," he groaned, "I need a shower."

Irene squeaked and then clapped a hand over her mouth. "I'm sorry," she said, muffled through her fingers.

Marcus looked up in surprise and dismissed her apology with a wave. Then he ran his fingers through his hair.

Irene studied her boss's face. "Something's changed about you."

Marcus looked up. "What do you mean?"

She shook her head. "I don't know, but time was, you wouldn't have minded that so much." She gestured toward the door.

"I guess that's true, but I became a Christian a few weeks ago."

Irene blinked and said nothing.

"Things are different now," Marcus continued. "Or they're supposed to be." He was contemplating with some surprise her claim that he had changed, and at the same time feeling guilty for his outburst at her. "I've still got a lot to work on. The language," he explained. "And the yelling. I'm really sorry about that."

Irene knitted her brows together and asked, "So does becoming a Christian mean you can't yell or cuss?"

Marcus answered almost without thinking. "It means that I realized I do all kinds of things I shouldn't do." He quirked his mouth to the side. "But it also means that I accepted God's gift of forgiveness, so eventually I can leave all that behind and enjoy perfection in eternity with Him." He shook his head. "I try to do better now, but..." he trailed off and looked down.

After a moment of silence, Irene reached out and patted him on the knee. "I think you're doing all right." Then she withdrew her hand, got up, and made her way out to her desk, leaving Marcus to gape after her.

9

Marcus did in fact shower when he got home later that afternoon, and then wasted it by heading to the basketball court, hoping the physical workout would help to clear his mind.

Forty-five minutes later he collapsed on the bench. As he downed a bottle of water, his phone pinged. It was Daniel, asking if he'd like to hit the courts.

Marcus chuckled to himself and then typed back,

Sure, why not?

By the time his friend arrived, he was recuperated and ready to go again. They warmed up together and then engaged in a battle of *21*, which Marcus won with no problem.

"Dang, dude, you were intense out there." Daniel offered this grudging praise as they cooled down.

"Sorry, man." Marcus said. "It's been a day."

"Yeah?"

As they took turns shooting haphazardly toward the basket, he told Daniel what had happened in his office that afternoon with Abigail. Almost as an afterthought, he added the conversation with Irene. At that Daniel stopped shooting and turned to look at him.

"What?" Marcus asked.

Daniel spun the ball in his hands. "You see what happened there, don't you?"

Marcus shook his head.

"You just witnessed to Irene."

Marcus stared at him in shocked silence. He'd been so busy brooding over his own failures that he hadn't stopped to think about that. "I guess," he said. "But it was probably negated by my actions."

Daniel gave him a look. "When did Irene say you were different? Before or after you yelled at her?"

Marcus dipped his head to one side. "After."

"Mm hmm." Daniel walked up to Marcus and stopped right in front of him. "It's not about doing everything perfectly. It's about how you handle yourself in an imperfect situation." He smacked the ball into Marcus's chest. "I've gotta git. Honey-do list tonight." He turned to grab his bag off the bench. "See ya."

"Yeah," Marcus said. "See ya."

He contemplated his friend's words all through the short drive home, and the second shower, and his solitary meal. It wasn't until his head sank into the pillow several hours later that the loneliness of not having a honey-do list hit him in the same spot the basketball had earlier that evening but with a much heftier punch.

1

Corinne was exhausted. Taking care of her injured parents was hard physical labor, something she was not used to. But it was also satisfying in a fundamental sort of way. Their needs were real and life-altering, and Corinne felt as though she were being useful, which was a pleasant sensation. Plus—and Corinne had not expected this either—she found herself enjoying the reconnection with her family on a deeper level than a short weekend visit could offer.

All in all, the time at home was good, even though she slept little and labored much. It wasn't only the needs of her parents creating the demand on her time. Not long after the accident, Casey delivered her third baby in five years. Guess who got to take care of the siblings?

She loved them like crazy, but they were an around-the-clock job. She'd never say it out loud, but she was relieved when her sister came home from the hospital and her own role downgraded to helper.

Everything else in her life was relegated to a waiting list. She had almost no time to spend on her business, but thankfully, between the understanding of her clients and the willingness of her contractors, it suffered little under her emaciated work schedule.

Her new prayer life was non-existent. She was asleep as soon as her head hit the pillow every night, and somehow, she just didn't have time to think about it during the day, during the endless stream of activity required to care for two immobile patients.

And of course she had no social life, unless you called the stream of people coming in and out with food and extra sets of helping hands, socializing.

No, the reality was that for weeks she thought of nothing other than what task was next on the to-do list. But eventually her parents regained strength, and Casey and her husband carved out a new family routine. Every moment that was freed up from all the intensive hands-on duty, Corinne began repurposing into her own normal routines, realizing as she did so just how much different her life had been these last two months, and how disconnected she was from her life in Sutton.

When the time came at long last that she didn't fall asleep the instant her head hit the pillow, she lay still, savoring the deliciousness of the feeling. Then she grabbed her phone and opened the Bible app.

"Hello," she murmured. After skimming through her long unused bookmarks, she laid the phone down on her stomach, feeling the disconnect with God, too. "I feel like I've been away forever, Lord." The reality of how easily that had happened washed over her.

"I'm sorry," she said. Her prayer that night felt like she was getting to know God all over again.

One not-so-welcome return to normality was when her parents found themselves feeling well enough to start worrying about their single daughter living in her old bedroom. Just about the time they started talking up the merits of the nice young man at church with two young children, Corinne began feeling antsy to return home.

Home! To her utter surprise, the image was of her little house, and her small-town church, and her close-knit group of friends, all of which were to be found in Sutton. At least, the friends had been close before the accident. To be sure, Becky reached out regularly by text the entire time Corinne was away, but the conversations were always short and focused on how her parents were doing. It's all Corinne could manage. Daniel sometimes said hello through his wife. Marcus had been silent.

In the returning spaces of time that Corinne had for pondering, she wondered about that. Of course, she hadn't reached out either, but she felt like she had a pretty good excuse. What was his? Why was he silent? Was it the same reason he hadn't been willing to make eye contact that last Sunday? Under the circumstances, she thought he might have asked about her parents. Then again, they hadn't had a chance to resolve anything, and he'd been pretty dark when they'd last spoken. With no answers, she lifted the situation up to God as she got back to praying. And she knew that once she returned home, one way or another they'd have to sort it out.

There it was again. Home. It was crazy that she felt this way; she'd been back in Indianapolis longer than she'd been there. How could it be home?

And yet it was.

As welcome and gratifying as that certainty was, Corinne felt no small amount of nervousness at the prospect of returning and having that conversation with Marcus. She had no idea what to expect or even what to say. Nevertheless, it didn't outweigh her anticipation of being back where she belonged.

She didn't rush it, though. She wanted to be sure her parents were ready to manage on their own before she took off.

The time finally came when she found herself with a free evening. After her third wandering pass through the house, her mother said, "Why don't you go see Evelyn? I know she'd love to visit with you in person."

"That's a good idea. I think I'll do it." Corinne dropped a kiss atop her mother's head and scooted out of the room to call her friend.

2

Corinne parked in the driveway of the modest brick home. Before she could ring the bell, Evelyn threw open the door. "I'm so glad you called! It's not often we get to talk in person." Corinne stepped inside the entryway and Evelyn wrapped her in a huge embrace. She then leaned back to assess. "You look well."

"Thank you! I'm getting more sleep now." She shrugged off her jacket and Evelyn hung it on a peg.

"That must mean your parents are healing?"

"They are! In fact, I think I've worn out my usefulness here."

"Hmm. Well, come sit down. We're going to eat cookies and talk all about it."

Evelyn led the way into a cozy living room. Two overstuffed armchairs stood opposite a worn but well-cared-for sofa. Corinne sank into its cushions while Evelyn poured two cups of tea. She handed one to Corinne and then offered her a platter of cookies.

'Ooh, chocolate chip! My favorite." Corinne selected two.

As they nibbled and sipped, Corinne brought her friend up to date on her parents' progress, Casey's family, and her own shifting responsibilities.

"And you feel the time is drawing near to return home?"

Evelyn's use of the word *home* to describe Ohio touched Corinne. "Yes." She hesitated, realizing she hadn't told Evelyn any of the latest about what took place in Sutton. "Oh, boy. There's a lot I need to catch you up on." Corinne told her about the business meeting and what she had learned about Marcus's past.

"Oh, my."

"Yeah." Corinne took a sip of tea as Evelyn contemplated what she'd just heard.

"You did the right thing, pointing him toward God."

"I guess. But then I dropped the ball. I haven't been praying for him since I got here."

"Why not?"

"I haven't been praying at all. It took me a while to even realize it."

"Your life has been pretty intense these past several weeks," Evelyn observed.

"But that doesn't make it okay."

Evelyn bobbed her head to the side. "Our faith journeys aren't perfect. The important thing is what you did about it once you realized." She raised her eyebrows.

Corinne gave her a half-hearted smile. "I started praying again."

"Exactly," Evelyn said, and sipped her tea.

"All right, I get that." Corinne reached for a third cookie and bit into it, deep in thought. Evelyn stayed quiet, and for a few moments the only sounds came from the outside world, cars passing by, kids playing in the yard next door, and a few hardy crickets chirping their last for the season.

"What if I can't handle it, Evelyn?"

"Your emotions, you mean?"

Corinne nodded.

"Well, coming home to Indianapolis gave you a break from them. In a way, that was a gift. You've had time away to develop perspective."

"What do you mean?"

"Your emotions aren't as raw as they were, right?" Corinne shook her head. "Having that break from them strengthens your ability to speak and think and make decisions from a better place."

Corinne had not considered this before. It almost felt wrong to think of her parents' accident as a means to an end in her own life. Still though. It was one good thing that came from that horrible event. "I guess I can see that. I still feel like I failed, though."

"How so?"

"I totally misread everything about the situation." She ducked her head. "Then when the truth came out, I was crushed. I should have been more careful."

Evelyn set down her cup. "Emotions are a tough thing. They happen. Having them isn't a failure." Corinne just looked at her. "Don't be too hard on yourself for not knowing the truth sooner. God allowed you to know it when it pleased Him to do so. That timing allowed you to witness to Marcus."

"I guess."

"And don't underestimate God's ability to put our meager offerings to use. Being willing to serve Him, and acting on that willingness, pleases God. Failure would be to refuse, and you haven't done that."

Corinne ran her index finger around the rim of her empty teacup. She still had to walk the path that God had for her, though, and it wasn't guaranteed to be easy.

As if she'd read her mind, Evelyn said, "Remember, God doesn't expect perfection from us. He just wants us to walk with Him."

Corinne leaned her head against the soft throw blanket that covered the back of the couch. Evelyn knew her well. Whenever Corinne undertook a task, she always wanted to do it perfectly. It wasn't easy redefining success as obedience instead of a particular outcome. She had to admit, though, that it would be way less stressful to leave the outcome up to God.

"Thank you, Evelyn. You always say just what I need to hear."

"That's just me trying to be willing to act on what God calls me to do, same as you."

When the evening ended and Corinne had donned her jacket, Evelyn reached out to hug her. "I'm so glad we had this opportunity, Corinne."

"Me too! I don't know what I would do without you."

It was nearly midnight when Corinne returned to her parents' home. She took a long hot shower and contemplated her conversation with Evelyn. If a life of faithful obedience wasn't about achieving certain goals, what was it about? How did she gauge her success? She turned this way and that, letting the spray hit every part of her neck and shoulders. *Obedience isn't doing nothing*, she thought. *On the contrary, it's very active.*

As the minutes ticked by and the water turned from hot to warm, and then tepid, Corinne decided that it must be about staying the course. Putting one foot in front of the other on the path toward Christ even when you didn't understand—or agree.

She turned off the water and stepped out of the shower. She dried the water droplets from her hair and brushed her teeth at the old standalone sink in the single bathroom of her parents' house. Then she padded down the hallway toward her bedroom and snuggled into bed. It was the same twin she'd slept in during high school.

She read a little in her Bible, said a prayer, and then turned over on her side. This life of faith, it might be a process, and it might be about obedience, but it still did have one absolute goal. A goal that was only achieved when you reached the end of your physical life here on earth. *Important to remember that,* Corinne thought. Then she fell asleep.

3

The gray light of predawn had just begun to seep in around the edges of the curtains in Corinne's room by the time she opened her eyes that next Saturday morning. "Good morning, Lord," she whispered.

She slipped out of bed and padded down the hall and through the house to the back door. She unlocked it and stepped out onto the deck, surveying the site of years of childhood play.

Corinne and her sister had befriended their fair share of urban wildlife within the confines of this cozy space. Trees and bushes provided a safe haven. A fence provided security. And their parents' willingness to embrace a little backyard chaos gave the two girls license to explore and build and imagine to their hearts' content.

One by one birds began filling the morning with song. The sound washed over Corinne, and she recalled a different backyard. A different set of people. She relished the memory and inhaled, savoring the cool, damp air that would vanish with the sun. Then she leaned on the rail and basked in the moment.

The sun was fully up and doing its duty when she heard her mother rattling around in the kitchen, getting breakfast. The return of her ability to complete such a task independently was the final piece of the puzzle for Corinne.

It was time to go home.

The drive from Indianapolis to Sutton was only about four hours, but it was still after midnight when Corinne pulled into the driveway. Even though she had decided first thing that morning it was time to leave, she had managed to procrastinate the day away. There were so many odds and ends to be done! Like discussing one more topic of conversation with her mother. Or rocking her nephew to sleep one more time.

Her dad almost chucked her out the door at the end. His eyes were misty, though, as he pulled her to him for one final, fervent embrace. "Thank you, my dear," he whispered into her hair. "I don't know what we would have done without you."

Corinne sniffled against his shoulder, and her tears, which had been threatening all day, overflowed. When she pulled away, her throat was constricted, and her voice squeaked. "I love you guys."

"We love you too, honey," her mom said and wrapped her in a warm and comfortable embrace. "You drive safe, now. You hear?"

The familiar reminder was more sobering these days, and Corinne promised.

The dollhouse was dark when she arrived. It also had that musty smell of a place long uninhabited. She turned on all the lights, threw open the windows, and carted her bags to the bedroom. Then she reacquainted herself with her little home. It didn't take long.

Back in the kitchen, she pulled open the refrigerator door. Empty. The sight jolted her into the realization that the life she had known for the past two months was over. It was the hardest work she had ever done, and yet she wouldn't have traded being there for her family for anything.

Now, though, it was time to move forward into her own life once again, and to see what God had in store for her.

The prospect both thrilled and terrified her.

4

Becky's jaw dropped when Corinne slipped into the pew beside her the next morning.

After a moment of stunned paralysis, she grabbed Corinne and hugged her so tightly the poor girl could scarcely breathe. But Corinne didn't care. Becky's welcome sealed the deal. She was home.

Even Daniel squeezed her hand in greeting once Becky set her free. "Welcome home, stranger!"

Then she saw movement over Daniel's shoulder. Marcus was in church! Corinne felt her whole body vibrate with the perfectness of it. She leaned forward to catch his eye, and she raised her hand in unaffected greeting.

He returned the gesture automatically, surprise evident in his features, and then he looked down.

"Girl," Becky whispered, tucking her arm through Corinne's and pulling her close. "I can't tell you how much I've missed you!"

Corinne closed her eyes and squeezed Becky's arm. The music had begun, but she whispered back anyway, "Oh, Becky. Me, too."

Her friends, her pastor, her church family, they all welcomed her with open arms throughout the morning. During the prayer, Corinne silently thanked God for this community, something she'd never had in all her travels.

Becky didn't miss a beat after the last amen. "You have got to come over," she said. "We'll have lunch and spend the afternoon catching up."

"Oh gosh, Becky. I'm so sorry but I just can't, not yet." Becky almost looked traumatized. "I only got in late last night, and I've got so much to do. Plus, right now, I'm exhausted." *Sleep deprivation isn't the only way a person can be worn out,* she realized. *Emotion will do it, too.*

"Of course you are." This was Daniel coming to her rescue. "Come on, Bec. Give the girl some time to breathe; she just got home!" He put his arm around his wife's shoulder and winked at Corinne. She couldn't help smiling. How she had missed Daniel, too.

Becky pursed her lips in a pout. "Oh, all right. But soon! Promise?"

"I promise." Corinne's eyes crinkled as she hugged her friend again.

And there, over Becky's shoulder was Marcus again, standing beside Daniel. Silent. Serious. As she caught his eye again, she smiled. He couldn't help but return it. Then he dipped his head briefly and mouthed the words, "Welcome home."

Still in Becky's embrace she silently replied, "Thank you."

It was then that her fellow worshippers engulfed her in a flood of greeting. She moved but slowly toward the exit and was among the last of the cars to leave the parking lot that morning. By the time she did, Daniel and Becky and Marcus had long since gone.

5

Her friends had honored her request for time to get her life back in order here in Sutton. By Monday evening she had a stocked refrigerator, clean laundry, and a full day of work under her belt.

She'd also had time to contemplate Marcus's presence in church. Totally not what she'd expected and discussed with Evelyn such a short time ago. But then again, he had said that church had turned his world upside down. Maybe he was seeking.

Uncertain what that meant for her but certain she was right where she belonged, Corinne dumped it all in God's lap during her prayers.

When the doorbell rang Monday evening, she was quite ready for visitors. Peeking out the window, she saw Marcus's car parked at the curb, and the old familiar lurch in her chest left her breathless. *What was this visit going to mean?*

"Steady, girl. Geez," she reproached herself, and grabbed the door handle to reinforce the command. Then she remembered to pray. "Help me to keep my eyes fixed on You, Lord."

She opened the door and there he stood. Tall, dark, and more fit than he had been two months ago. She hadn't noticed that at church. His black, wavy hair still fell stubbornly across his forehead. She loved that.

"Hi," she said.

"Hello." He grinned crookedly. "Sorry to bother you. I know you're just getting settled in again, but I owe you this." He produced an envelope she hadn't noticed and held it out to her.

"You're not bothering me. It didn't take long to get everything going." She took the envelope. "What is this?"

"Payment," he said. "For working on the Fredrickson case."

"Oh!" Corinne was embarrassed. "I guess not everything's going. My own books aren't caught up yet."

"Cobbler's kids have worn out shoes?" he asked.

"Yeah, exactly." She set the envelope on the little table by the door. "Thank you for this."

"You're welcome." Then he rushed on. "Listen, I'm sorry I never asked about your parents while you were gone." His eyes filled with uncertainty. "I didn't know if you'd want to hear from me."

Corinne melted a little bit at those words. He could be cocky and self-assured, and then in the very next heartbeat, broken and insecure. It was a bit of a roller coaster ride, but Corinne didn't mind that. It was real and honest.

"It's okay, Marcus. If you want to know the truth, even Becky could barely get more than two words out of me at a time. It was crazy busy there."

"I figured it was. I can't even imagine."

After a moment of silence, Corinne asked, "Would you like to come in?"

Marcus's face registered surprise. "Are you sure? I mean, I'd love to talk." He gestured to the side. "How about we sit out here? It's a nice evening."

"Sounds good to me." Corinne stepped out the door and pulled it shut behind her. They sat in the two deck chairs, and a brief, awkward silence descended upon them.

Then Marcus said, "So how are they? Your parents?"

"Oh! I guess I didn't answer that before, did I?"

"I don't think I asked before," Marcus replied, and then smiled at the surprised look on Corinne's face.

"Come to think of it, I guess you didn't. Well, they're doing fine. Mom made breakfast yesterday morning." Her eyes misted over at the memory. "That's when I knew it was time to come home."

Marcus took in a long, slow, deep breath when she said the word "home". It set all his nerves tingling, and all he could do was watch her.

Coming out of her reverie, Corinne looked over at him. "It was good to see you in church yesterday."

If she hadn't known the man previously, she would have thought him incredibly shy, the way he was behaving. He looked down at his hands. "I've kept going."

"That's good."

"Yeah. I guess I belong there." Marcus hesitated for a moment and then rushed on. "I've been going to a men's Bible study, too. It's good. And there's a prayer group that meets once a week in the morning. Plus, I'm still having breakfast with Roger on Mondays. You knew about that, right?" He looked up at her.

Corinne shook her head, reeling from this very churchy list of Marcus's activities.

"Oh. He's been great. Right after you left, I was kind of a mess." He stopped and thought about that. "Well, I was a mess before you left, too." He watched her, trying to gauge her response. It was the first opportunity they'd had to talk since that last disastrous meeting in his office, and he still wasn't sure how she'd respond.

What she did was raise her eyebrows in encouragement. She had that look of warmth and caring that always caught him off guard when he was expecting anger. It gave him strength, and so he continued.

"My whole life has been a mess. I feel like the only thing I ever got right was my law degree. Anyway, when you left it felt like just one more in a long line of screw-ups. Only this time, something was different..."

He stared off into space for a moment. Corinne kept silent and just watched him. She felt jittery as she wondered what might be coming.

Marcus went on. "Roger and Daniel both helped me a lot. Daniel explained what it means to be a Christian, and Roger took me through the passages of Scripture and helped me pray."

Corinne blinked. She opened her mouth and then closed it again. *Is he saying what I think he's saying?* She tipped her head and said, "Tell me about that."

"He helped me pray to accept Jesus as my Savior." Marcus drew in a deep breath. "These past two months have been crazy since then. I feel like for every single thing I learn about being a Christian, I find five others that I'm clueless about."

Corinne's jaw dropped as the actual words registered. "Marcus, that's amazing!"

He eyed her. "What, that I'm clueless?" In that moment the old teasing look on his face returned.

"Pfft, no! That you became a Christian and are getting to know God. That is what's amazing. And wonderful." She reached out and snatched his hand, giving it a squeeze. "Oh, my gosh! Welcome to the family!" Then she just as quickly withdrew.

Marcus was touched beyond measure. "Thank you," he said.

They both fell silent again, each lost in their thoughts, each with much to contemplate.

Marcus was the first to surface, because he still carried burdens which he very much wished to lay down.

"Corinne, there's more I need to say." She looked over at him, still deep in her own thoughts. Marcus pushed ahead. "I owe you an apology for how I behaved at our last meeting." He looked down at his hands again, ashamed as he thought of it. "I honestly don't know why I was such an ogre, but I'm sorry for it. Will you forgive me?"

When Corinne didn't respond, he grew worried and peered up at her. She had those warm, crinkly eyes and a bit of a smile on her lips. Just waiting for him to look up. "Of course."

The relief was evident on Marcus's face. "Thank you," he said.

"I think I know why," she said.

Marcus was confused. "Why what?"

"Why you were such an ogre."

Marcus blinked, not sure he wanted to hear it, but not wanting to not hear it, either. "Okay," he said.

"From everything you've told me and all our interactions since we met last spring, I believe God has been pursuing you."

"You've said that before."

"Yes. And maybe your explosion that day had to happen to open the way for Him to come in. Sometimes He has to use the tough stuff in order to get through to us."

The idea was a sobering one for Marcus.

Corinne continued. "There's a verse in Romans that says, 'All things work together for the good of those who love God.' All things, both the good and the bad. If God used that difficult meeting to bring you to Him, then it was one hundred percent worth it."

Marcus's eyes began to water. He couldn't comprehend it. All those weeks she'd been gone, when they hadn't had closure. All his agonizing over whether she hated him, whether she'd return, whether there was any chance for him at all.

And what she saw was God at work.

"You're amazing," he said.

She scoffed. "I am not."

"Yes, you are. All the stuff you know about faith. And you always know just the right thing to say to point the way to God."

"Oh." Corinne was thoughtful. "I don't, though. God's been doing a lot of work in me these last few months, too." She drew in a deep shuddering breath and blew it out. "Things have happened here that have never happened before, and most of the time I feel like I'm clueless. I must be a slow learner." She shook her head in embarrassment.

"His timing though, right?"

She couldn't help but agree. "His timing. I guess I shouldn't fuss."

"You shouldn't." His smile this time was the one filled with a sincerity and warmth that reached all the way to his eyes and magnetized her to him. Corinne liked that serious side of him, too. A lot. *Perhaps—well, best not to think of it.* She sent a prayer upward for God to help her stay focused on Him.

The next few moments of companionable silence soon gave way to more discomfort for Marcus. He still had one more topic to address, and he had no idea how to do it. Almost without thinking, he also lifted a silent prayer to God for help.

"There's one more thing I need to tell you. Oh, I don't know how to do this." He took a deep breath and blew it out. "I want to tell you about my life. My relationships. Is that okay?"

She nodded mutely.

"First, I wasn't trying to keep it from you. It's a hard thing to know when to bring it up. But I also never meant to bring it up like I did." He huffed and shook his head. "We've already covered that. The truth is I've always just wanted to be married, which is probably surprising given how messed up my parents' marriage was." He ran his fingers through his hair. "Or maybe it contributed; I don't know. I just know I wanted somebody to live life with. But somehow the girls I ended up with—dated, married—they developed some expectation of me that I couldn't fulfill, and things got nasty."

He looked up at her. "I didn't want to recreate my parents' life. I see enough of that kind of stuff in my job. Too much probably." He looked thoughtful for a moment. "Anyway, I never had a clue how to make it better, so I walked away."

Marcus and Corinne sat in silent contemplation for a few moments. Corinne's heart ached for whatever chaos Marcus had lived through as a child, and how it had affected him as an adult. Whatever difficulties she may have experienced paled in comparison.

She was startled back to the present when Marcus continued his story. "The first one was right out of high school. She wasn't pregnant." He shot her a glance. "We just wanted to be together. What we didn't realize was that two high school diplomas couldn't provide her with the same lifestyle she'd been accustomed to growing up. It didn't take long for her to decide that she preferred that lifestyle and start nagging for it." Marcus looked over at Corinne. "I couldn't provide it. We lasted two whole months before I ran."

"Ouch."

"Yeah." He exhaled. "But you know, the second one was much the same. Right out of college. I was headed to law school, so still poor. She had her degree and went to work, but she was ready for "the good life" that two incomes would provide." He made air quotes to emphasize his point. "Instead, we never saw each other because I was always studying, or working some part-time job."

Marcus shook his head. "If we'd stayed married, I would have pursued a corporate position in the city—and hated it. We'd still never have seen each other, but we would've had the lifestyle she wanted. I guess three years was just too long to wait for it and she started pushing me. I'm not sure what she expected me to do..."

Marcus stared at nothing, his face bleak. "I didn't know what to do, so I walked away. Again. I think I married the same kind of girl both times. What an idiot."

Corinne held up a hand. "Not necessarily. That happens sometimes. People are attracted to a certain type of person.

Plus, you've got to remember, those relationships were before you knew God. You didn't have Him to guide you."

Marcus looked at this woman sitting next to him. Her expression was serious and earnest. She believed what she was telling him. Then a surprising thought occurred to him. As much as he had always loved to banter—and still did—he found himself hooked on deep conversations like these with her, too. He could see himself being hooked for a lifetime. *Perhaps—well, best not to think of it.*

Instead, he said, "You see? That's what I'm talking about. You always know the right thing to say."

Corinne huffed, but her countenance showed that she was pleased. Marcus liked that.

"So, what about us?" he blurted out.

Her face changed in an instant to surprise.

"Well, not *us*, exactly," he back-pedaled, embarrassed and kicking himself for ruining the moment. "I mean the two people that are you and me. Are we okay after all this?"

Are we okay? Corinne leaned back in her chair as she thought about it. *We dealt with the issues that were left hanging this summer, and we're still talking. There's so much we don't know about each other, but I love learning every new thing about him. Maybe—*

She tapped her upper lip with her index finger. Then her eyes changed and took on a bit of the twinkle that so captivated Marcus. "I think," she said, "that the two people who are you and me are sitting in my new deck chairs and talking together." Then she leaned forward. "And I like it."

Marcus thought this over, a slow smile spreading across his face. "I like it, too," he said. Then he gave the arm rest a pat and grinned wickedly at her. "And these deck chairs are the best!"

Corinne's eyes widened in surprise. Then her head dropped forward, and her shoulders shook with silent, but delighted, laughter.

About the Author

"She lights up when she talks about her writing!"

That's what happens when you finally achieve a lifelong goal.

Chantal DeYoe has been writing since she could hold a pencil, but it wasn't until recently that her journey brought her to where she could complete her first full-length fiction novel.

For decades Chantal has dedicated her life to whatever God has brought her way: homeschooling, piano, non-profit work, building a business. In all these things, He has been preparing her for this new path of writing and publishing.

Chantal loves to laugh and enjoy life, but she is also a deep thinker who loves getting inside the minds of her characters. She and her husband have two grown sons who've flown the coop, leaving them to live in rural Ohio with lots of animals—and plenty of small towns nearby.

Acknowledgements

My heartfelt thanks to my family and friends for their support of my work on this book. To my editor Caryn and my cover designer Lynn, thank you! To the social media community who so readily share knowledge and encouragement to all who undertake the daunting task of self-publishing, I am grateful.

Coming Soon!

Not What They Expected (working title)

Sutton Series Book 2

www.chantaldeyoe.com